SEER

Rendezvous with God – Volume Five

Bill Myers

T0282978

FIDELIS
PUBLISHING

Discussion questions have been included
to facilitate personal and group study.

Fidelis Publishing®
Winchester, VA • Nashville, TN
www.fidelispublishing.com

ISBN: 9781956454574
ISBN: 9781956454581 (ebook)

Seer: A Novel
Rendezvous with God Volume Five
Copyright © 2024 Bill Myers

(NIV) New International Version®, NIV® Scripture comes from Holy Bible, Copyright ©1973, 1978, 1984, 2011 by Biblica, Inc.® Used by permission. All rights reserved worldwide.

Order at www.faithfultext.com for a significant discount. Email info@ fidelispublishing.com to inquire about bulk purchase discounts.

Published in association with Amaris Media International

Cover designed by Diana Lawrence
Interior layout/typesetting by Lisa Parnell
Edited by Amanda Varian

Manufactured in the United States of America

10 9 8 7 6 5 4 3 2 1

Derrick Warfel
Humble hero of the faith

Let my heart be broken by the things that break Your heart.

—David Livingstone, Scottish missionary

PART ONE

CHAPTER
ONE

DON'T ASK ME which came first, the pounding in my head or the *hiss-click* of the hospital respirator. It doesn't matter. Both were minor league players compared to the searing pain in my gut.

Am I dead? I thought.

"Please," came the reply, "my reward program is better than that."

I recognized the humor and tried opening my eyes. But they were sealed so tight I had to raise my eyebrows to pull them open. When I succeeded, the brightness was blinding. I squinted until it dimmed into details of an ICU room—beeping machine above and to my right, a bedside table pushed aside to my left. Beyond it, the smallest of windows. And beside me, in a chair wearing his trademark robe and sandals, sat Yeshua—casually reading a book.

I tried speaking but my mouth was dry as sand. My throat, raw hamburger—the tubes running into my nose and down didn't help.

So, I thought, *I'm alive?*

Yeshua glanced up, smiling. "Can't pull anything over on you."

How? I scowled. *Back at the prison. You gave me a choice. Free will . . . I said I was ready to go and . . . and . . .*

"That's what your mouth said. But your heart had other ideas. Blame Siggy, he's the one who tipped your hand."

I closed my eyes recalling how my golden retriever refused to leave my graveside service. It hadn't been a dream or vision. It was more like one of Yeshua's multiple dimension things—watching my possible funeral in my possible future which, apparently, never occurred. I re-opened my eyes and thought, *The prison riot—the guy with the knife.*

"Hate," he sadly shook his head. "It brings such suffering."

You have no idea, I thought until I spotted his hands. The shiny scar tissue filling the holes always stopped me. I changed subjects. *What are you reading?*

"Your book."

My book?

"Volume Four."

Volume Four? I never finished the first one.

"Not yet."

Before I could respond, I noticed movement to the left. With effort, I turned my head to see someone standing on the bed railing above me. Not sitting. *Standing.* He leaped into the air and landed on my bedside table—in a handstand! First two hands, then one. The only thing more bizarre than his action was his appearance—flowing blonde hair and a sculptured torso clad in a white gymnast leotard.

Drugs, I thought. *Definitely the drugs.*

"Nope."

Then what . . . Who is he!?

"My partner."

Your partner! From what I'd read, Jesus Christ had no partners—unless you counted the Father, which this person definitely was not. Or . . . I watched as the gymnast leaped from the table, simultaneously snatching a printed form off it, and lighting upon the small nurse's cabinet near the foot of my bed. *That's not . . .*

Yeshua looked on with amusement while the gymnast somersaulted in the air landing on one hand while folding the form with another.

Is that . . . the Holy Spirit?

Yeshua chuckled. "Only as you see him. Actually, it's not a bad interpretation. Artistic, creative. Energetic." Shaking his head in amusement he added, "And he does like to stay busy."

The gymnast had folded the paper into an origami bird and tossed it to Yeshua who caught it with a grin.

What is that? I asked.

"It was your DNR."

My . . . ?

"Do Not Resuscitate."

I blinked.

"I know it's a lot to take in. For now it's best you get a little rest. We'll have plenty to do soon enough."

To do? We're not done?

Yeshua smiled and tossed the origami toward the window. It flapped its wings and flew across the room, effortlessly passing through the glass into the bright morning sky. Only then did I notice the grisly giant of a soldier standing at attention next to the window. He had a jagged scar, from his left eye down to his jaw. Besides wearing battle fatigues, he was decked out with more weapons than a Texas gun show.

Wait. Who's that?

Closing the book, Yeshua said, "Your battalion commander."

My—

"Protection detail." Smiling, he turned from the soldier to me. "Really? That's how you see him?"

I didn't answer but was looking past the soldier to the dozens of similarly dressed men floating just outside. *Are those, are they like—angels? What about the feathers, wings? Where are their swords?*

"Don't blame me; it's *your* interpretation."

I stared a moment then turned back to him. *And you?* I thought. *Are you also my interpretation?*

"If I didn't appear as a man you wouldn't talk to me as a man."

I saw the real you once, didn't I? On the mountain with Moses and Elijah.

"So terrifying that you, Peter, and the guys all did face-plants."

I never felt such fear.

"Exactly. It's hard to carry on a conversation when everyone's groveling face-first in the dirt. Well," he said, rising, "we have plenty to do. And a brand-new book to work on."

Another adventure?

"Your best yet."

You always say that.

"Have I ever lied?" He had me there. "What do you think all your training has been about?"

My training? For what?

"In time. For now, you need to get some rest."

At least tell me where I'm going?

"If I did you'd just get out of the car and try to push." With a twinkle he added, "And we've both seen how well that works."

Right, but—

"Sleep."

But . . . My eyes fluttered then closed. They did not reopen for thirty-six hours.

❧

"Please, Uncle Will . . ."

As I drifted back into consciousness, I recognized the voice.

"Stop being so selfish. My birthday's next week."

And the attitude.

I forced open my eyes to see the same ICU. Only now, at the side of my bed, was Amber, my fourteen-year-old niece—hunched over, small and helpless, "I need you. Me and Billie-Jean. Please . . ."

Despite the weight of the IV port, I moved my hand, actually just my fingers, until they touched hers.

Startled, she looked up. "Uncle Will?"

I tried to smile.

Wiping the streams of mascara from her face, she cried, "You're awake!"

The smile would still not come.

"It's a miracle!" she cried. "A miracle!"

I closed my eyes and slept. Enough excitement for one week.

CHAPTER
TWO

MY FIRST DAY out of ICU and they all filed in—Amber, Chip (her seventeen-year-old boyfriend), and Darlene, my outspoken and occasionally profane friend who became Amber's surrogate mother. Only Patricia was missing.

"Hey, Will." Chip gave me a thumbs-up as he entered. As an Olympian butt-kisser, he added, "Looking good."

Darlene had a different take. "You look like crap." Then, in surprising candor, she asked, "You doing okay?"

"They—" I coughed, my throat still like sandpaper. "They say my scar is really sexy."

"You'll be a babe magnet," Chip said, flipping back his hair and flashing a smile. I didn't bother returning it.

"You got everyone talking," Amber said. "You're all over social media."

Darlene sighed. "Once again."

Some habits are hard to break.

"How cool is it," Chip said, "some old-timer starting a prison riot over the injustices of our criminal system."

I wanted to explain that wasn't exactly how it happened, but that would imply knowing more than the news media, let alone a seventeen-year-old—both I'd learned to be impossible.

"You had us worried there for a while," Darlene said.

"Not me," Amber said. "I prayed."

"Actually, babe," Chip said, "we all prayed."

"*All?*" I threw a glance to Darlene.

She shrugged. "Any port in a storm."

"You even made the Trevor Hunter show," Amber said.

I frowned.

Chip explained, "That talk-show preacher guy? He says you're like a role model, a real hardcore hero."

My frown deepened.

"He believes in miracles too," Amber said. "Like what happened to Billie-Jean. We watch him a lot, don't we, babe."

"You bet," Chip said.

I gave Darlene a questioning look.

She shook her head indicating, *Kids, what can you do.*

So—" I cleared my throat, "how is Billie-Jean?"

"The picture of health," Chip said.

Amber added, "Cause she's a baby, they won't let her in the hospital, so Patricia, she's staying behind to watch her."

"Always the martyr," Darlene muttered.

We were interrupted by the quiet moan of my roommate—a frail fossil of man just this side of death. He'd been admitted the night before with severe abdominal pains. The heavy sedation didn't stop his occasional groans.

"Is he okay?" Amber asked. "What's wrong with him?"

I shook my head.

He gave another moan, more painful than the last.

"We should pray for him," Chip said. "What do you say, babe?"

"Absolutely," Amber agreed.

I turned back to Darlene who directed her gaze out the window. The two kids crossed over to the patient's bed then glanced to each other, unsure what to do.

"Put our hands on him?" Chip whispered. "Like they say on TV?"

It seemed a good idea. Amber reached out her hand and set it on the man's chest. He let out a quiet groan and she pulled away. After a moment, she settled for two fingers resting lightly on his arm.

"Uncle Will," she asked, "you want to join us?"

Darlene rose and headed for the door. "I'll be in the hall."

"Uncle Will?"

"Uh," I swallowed, "okay."

"Go ahead," she said, "you start."

"Out loud?"

"Sure," Chip said. "You're the seasoned pro, right?" Oddly, there was no irony in his voice. Instead, he bowed his head and closed his eyes. Amber did the same and waited. I nervously cleared my throat. Don't get me wrong, I'm a big fan of prayer. Particularly after Yeshua's lengthy lesson with Billie-Jean. But out loud? Not that I was ashamed. Hadn't I just taught a Bible study in prison (*that started a riot against the injustice of our criminal system*)? And I was fine saying grace over meals which, let's face it, was just rote. But the few times I tried improvising without a script, it seemed I was always listening to myself—self-conscious, like it was a performance for others.

"Um, listen," I cleared my voice again. "My throat still hurts." I coughed and winced to make my point. "You two go ahead. I'll just lay here and agree."

Amber opened one eye at me. "You sure?"

"Yeah." I gave another cough to close the deal. "I'm good."

"Alright . . ." But there was something about her tone that said she knew better—a gift she was developing by hanging out with Patricia and Darlene.

Fortunately, and to prove there was a loving God in heaven, we were interrupted by the nurse—a stout, forty-ish woman with thick arms, and the bedside manner of a boot-camp sergeant. "Visiting hours are over," she said. "Wrap it up."

"But we were just going to pray," Amber said.

"Take it outside, honey. The boys here need their beauty rest."

Amber turned to me. "Uncle Will?"

I nodded, indicating that as a professional, the woman knew best.

"It will only take a second," Chip argued. "If we could just—"

She turned to him and he stopped. "I'm sorry," her voice was an octave lower. "Did I not make myself clear?"

Chip swallowed.

She waited.

Gathering whatever manhood he had, and proving it by wrapping a protective arm around Amber, he herded her toward the door. "Let's go, babe."

"Bye, Uncle Will," Amber said. "Maybe we'll come by tomorrow."

I smiled and nodded.

Chip gave another thumbs-up. "Take care, dude."

I managed to retain the smile.

As they exited, my roommate let out another groan, more like a cry. It lasted longer than normal before it faded into a whimpering sigh—one that haunted me for the rest of the night.

CHAPTER
THREE

I WOKE TO the sound of voices.

"Dad?" A woman was speaking. "If you can hear us, we love you."

A little girl's voice cracked, "I love you, Grandpa."

I turned toward the heavy curtain now drawn between my roommate and myself.

The woman continued, "But if you want to leave, if the pain is too great . . ." She choked on the words and came to a stop.

A man's voice joined in. "We want you to fight it, Dad, but if it's too much, we understand."

Yeshua's voice spoke. "Heartbreaking, isn't it?"

I turned to see him on the other side of my bed, head lowered, dark hair falling over his face.

"There's no way to help?" I asked.

He looked up, eyes rimmed with red. "Just one."

Of course, I knew what he meant. Not because of my mini-cowardness the day before with Amber and Chip.

And not because of my roomie's groans during the night. But because I knew Yeshua—his love for the man, and his relentless desire for me to grow.

"What?" I argued. "You're saying if I prayed out loud for him something would have changed?"

"It still can."

I heard the little girl begin to cry.

"What?" I repeated. "You want me to pray for him now? With them?"

He said nothing which left me totally defenseless. I hate it when he does that. "*Go into your inner room*," I quoted. "*Close the door and pray to your Father in secret.*"

He smiled. "You *have* been reading."

"Prayer is a private thing."

"Until my love spills out of you onto others."

"Come on, that's not my style."

A gust of hot air hit my face, forcing me to close my eyes. When I reopened them, we were standing in a cave shaded by a large, spreading oak. At our feet lay a flat rectangle of smooth stone, five by six feet. It opened onto a narrow channel of rock leading to a smaller rectangle. From my research—and trust me, along with my reading, I'd been doing plenty—I guessed it to be a winepress. But it was dry. No grapes. No wine. Only a nearby pile of wheat stalks and the warm air smelling of dust.

Near the tree a skinny kid in his early twenties knelt. His shirt was off, revealing a body that could definitely stand a gym membership. But it was the big, burly soldier he was kneeling before who caught my attention.

"Where are we?" I whispered.

"You're the Bible reader," Yeshua said.

"It's a big book."

"You've checked out Judges? Gideon?"

Before I answered, the soldier spoke, a commanding voice full of gravel. "The Lord is with you, mighty warrior."

I scanned the cave, the winepress, the brute soldier, the skinny kid. "That's him?" I asked. "Gideon?"

"And the angel."

The soldier wore a battered helmet, leather armor, and a sword strapped to his side. Only then did I notice a familiar scar running from his left eye down to his jaw. "Is that . . ."

Yeshua nodded. "A different interpretation than yours, but yes." I stared as Yeshua continued. "Gideon is hiding out from his enemy, the Midianites, same as you."

I frowned. "There are no Midianites in my life."

"You have the same enemy."

"What are you talking about?"

"Like Gideon, you refuse to see yourself as I see you."

The kid spoke, his voice thinner. "But the Lord abandoned us. He turned us over to the Midianites."

Unimpressed, the soldier answered, "Go in the strength you have and save Israel from Midian."

"But—"

"Am I not sending you?" The soldier wasn't angry, but clearly not interested in chit-chat.

And Gideon? The kid was too terrified to argue but he was still trying to make sense of it. "How can I save Israel?" he asked. "My clan is the weakest in Manasseh, and I am the least in my family."

"You will strike down every Midianite, leaving none alive."

If the first statement was hard for him to grasp, this second was downright impossible.

I leaned to Yeshua and whispered, "You can't blame him for doubting, he's afraid."

"Like you."

I started to argue, but he had me—at least when it came to praying with Amber—and with a family of total strangers.

"Fear is only a symptom, Will. A weapon in the hands of the parasite."

"Parasite?"

"Not a bad description of Satan."

"I don't understand."

"Think about it. The devil can't create anything on his own. He can only twist and distort what I've already created—and what you've already given him."

"What *I've*—I've not given him anything."

"You've given him your identity."

"I've what? I'm God's child. You've said that a million times."

"Yet you keep giving away that belief."

"That's not true, I believe it."

"In your head." He reached over and tapped my chest. "But in here . . . ? It's all about your identity, Will. Whose words will you believe, mine or the parasite's?"

I looked over to the kid.

Yeshua continued, "Once Gideon accepts his identity, he'll accomplish everything I've promised—just like you."

"Just like—" I turned to him but was suddenly back in bed, the hot, dry air replaced by the hospital's AC. Yeshua had disappeared, but my gymnast friend had returned. He was stretched out at the foot of my bed, resting his head on one hand while using the other to quickly fashion a tiny, floating elephant—four inches tall with pink, feathery wings.

"Look who's back," I muttered.

We never leave, Yeshua's voice answered.

I watched as he swept the animal aside. It vaporized and he started another.

"He looks bored," I said.

He's just doodling. Waiting on you.

"Waiting on me—to step up and pray?"

No time like the present.

"And if I refuse?"

Free will is always an option, you know that.

I did know. But I also knew if I refused, we'd keep circling the mountain until his love had its way. For Yeshua, compassion always wins.

I turned to the quiet sobs on the other side of the curtain and hesitated. It was one thing to talk about God to inmates at the prison, that had been my job. But to completely broadside this family? Me, a total stranger? And what if it didn't work? What if—

The room filled with a strange smell. Something like burnt matches. I saw the middle of the curtain begin to bulge. It continued until a black, spindly arm poked through. It wasn't human. More like something from a cheesy, horror flick. It was covered in spines, shiny in slime from what looked like open lesions. Instead of fingers it had curved, razor-sharp talons—reaching out for me!

I gasped, pulling back—and probably letting out a little scream in the process—until a sword, not unlike Gideon's soldier's, appeared and sliced through the air severing the arm. I heard an ungodly shriek as it fell to the floor, both arm and sword evaporating before they hit.

"What was that?!" I don't know if I shouted it or thought it. It didn't matter.

Yeshua's reply was immediate. *Your fear.*

I stared wide-eyed at the curtain, my confidence not exactly bolstered. The fact it rippled again with multiple bulges followed by more talons poking through did not help. I threw a desperate look to the gymnast. He casually pushed aside his latest creation, a miniature bear with bunny ears—and suddenly exploded into blazing light. The power was unimaginable, reminding me of what I saw when I was in heaven. Impossibly intense. Full of terror—and love. For a moment I saw a pair of gigantic wings fill the room. I turned my head, sucking in my breath. But it wasn't just air I breathed. It was him. I felt him rushing into my throat, filling my lungs—then spreading throughout my body. As it did, as *he* did—and this is hard to describe—I felt my fear being pushed out, replaced by his presence.

It lasted only a moment before fading. I knew I better act now while the fear was still gone. I turned back to the curtain. The bulges and talons were gone.

"Excuse me?" I said. "Excuse me!"

The voices of the family on the other side stopped.

"May I . . ." I paused, fighting to sound less manic. "Do you mind . . . do you mind if I pray for him?"

There was silence. I suspect shared looks. Finally, the man cleared his voice, "All right . . . if you'd like."

Almost, before I could stop them, more words poured out of me. "Will you join me?"

This time there was no response.

And no surprise.

I turned back to the gymnast, who condensed to his more familiar form. My look to him made it clear I didn't know what to do. His look to me made it clear I did. I hesitated, took a deep breath, and in my best Charlton Heston, said: "And I say unto you . . ." Sadly, it quickly degenerated into Pee Wee Herman, "um, uh . . ."

I looked back to the gymnast who nodded. He'd done his job; apparently it was time for me to do mine. (Like Yeshua, he seemed no fan of enabling.)

I took another breath and tried again. "I say unto you to"—and another breath—"stop being sick." There I said it. I didn't exactly sound like the guys on TV, but close enough to feel like a fool.

And the response?

More of nothing. Except for whispered words on the other side of the curtain. "Nutjob . . . fanatic . . ."

I turned back to the gymnast whose hand was raised, counting down—first four fingers, then three, then two, then one and . . .

"Grandpa!" the little girl's voice cried. "Grandpa, you're awake!"

"Dad?" the woman said.

I heard coughing, a wheezing gasp.

"Dad, Dad are you alright?"

More coughing.

"Dad," the man said, "lie back down. Jenn, call the nurse!"

"Dad," the woman cried, "you're not well, you have to lie back—"

"It's okay, dear." Another voice spoke, male and much older. Faint but not feeble. "Everything's . . . it's okay. I'm . . . fine."

CHAPTER
FOUR

"COULD IT NOT simply have been a coincidence?" Patricia asked.

"I felt God wanted the guy healed. So I prayed and . . ."

"He was healed."

"Exactly." There were a few other details to share but this wasn't the time. What I really needed was context. And Patricia, with her years of training and experience in the mission field, was the closest I could find.

She grew silent as she wheeled me through the hospital's halls. The lights were lowered for the evening and the place was tranquil, almost surreal. I didn't mind her taking time to answer, she had a lot to digest. So did I.

Finally, she said, "And the family, they didn't thank you?"

"They couldn't wait to get him out of there." More silence. "Why do you find it so hard to believe it was a miracle? You've seen healings in your past. We all saw what happened with the baby, with Billie-Jean."

"Yes," she said. "But . . ."

"What about Joseph Namaliu, your friend from Papua New Guinea?"

"Yes . . ." She spoke carefully, as precise with her words as with every other detail in her life. "But Joseph has devoted his entire life to God. He was trained in seminary, teaches at universities and leading Bible colleges. There's no man or woman I know more committed to purity and holiness."

"And I'm a newbie, I get it. With lots of baggage."

She put up no argument.

We passed the nurse's station and turned right, heading down another hallway. "What about medication?" she asked. "Perhaps you were having a reaction. With your authorization I can check the charts to see—"

"Patricia—"

"It's a valid question. You were in surgery for hours. We nearly lost you—actually we did. And the violence you experienced in that prison—for all we know you could be experiencing a type of PTS."

"Post Traumatic Syndrome?"

"Stranger things have happened."

Stranger things? I had my doubts. But as I said there was no need to blow up her neat and tidy world with all that was happening to mine. We continued silently down the hall until a woman's voice softly called through the PA. "Code blue. Code blue."

I craned my head, looking up to Patricia. "Is that, is someone . . . ?"

She nodded. "Cardiac arrest." We slowed to a stop. Ahead, one of the little dome lights above each of the rooms was flashing.

I looked back up at Patricia. Her expression said it all. And with her look it dawned on me what I should do. I wasn't crazy about the idea, but I knew. "Wheel me in there," I said.

"Will." Her hesitancy was clear. But this was no time to argue. I gripped the rims of the wheels and pushed off from her. "Will!"

When I arrived at the door, I spotted a heavy, Latina woman in her fifties. She lay in the closest bed, the monitor beside her shrilly beeping. I entered the room and rolled to her side. From the next bed over a teen girl watched, eyes wide in alarm. But I'd not be put off. The first time I hesitated had nearly been a disaster. Not this time. Pushing aside my fear—and believe me I had plenty—I reached out, set my hands on the woman's chest and shouted over the alarm, "And I say unto you—"

"Will!"

I couldn't remember last night's wording but pressed ahead. "Heart, start beating!" It sounded a bit amateurish, so I threw in an extra, "Be healed!"

The alarm continued.

I spotted the teen raising her cell phone. Hearing commotion behind me, I turned to see two attendants rushing in, wheeling a crash cart. The bigger, a wannabe WWF wrestler—300 pounds if an ounce—shouted, "Sir!"

But I would not be intimidated. I turned back to the woman.

"Sir! Step aside!"

With all the urgency I could muster, I clenched my eyes and repeated, "Be healed!"

"Will!"

Someone grabbed my chair. I was dragged backward, replaced by the crash cart—the teen capturing it all on her phone.

"What's he doing here?" another voice demanded.

"Be healed!" I shouted.

"Get him out of here!"

They tried turning me toward the door, but I threw on the brakes. I would not be stopped. "Start beating!" I shouted. "Be healed! Be healed!"

The bigger man picked me up, chair and all. Swearing, he half-carried, half-dragged me past an angry doctor and into the hallway where Patricia stood, hand to mouth, staring in horror.

Was the woman healed?

Yes.

By me?

No.

Did Patricia have some very candid words to share?

We're talking Patricia Swenson, right?

But it wasn't her words that stung. It was Yeshua's betrayal. Hadn't I stepped in? Done exactly what he wanted? I saw the woman's need; I sucked it up and I obeyed. Mission accomplished. What more did he want?

ღ

The following morning, as I finished breakfast, two overly pleasant administrators swung by. One, a gentlemen in a wrinkled suit and oily combover, the other a woman in radiant white hair and an over-enthusiasm for Chanel No. 5. After comments on the weather and did I find my room suitable, they got down to business.

"Dr. Thomas," the woman forced a smile as she pulled large, black-rimmed glasses from her pocket. Slipping them on, she looked down at her yellow, legal pad. "After reviewing your interference with the hospital staff last night—"

"Serious interference," Combover added.

"Yes, serious," she said. "Not to mention your harassment of the patient—"

"Hold it," I interrupted. "Harassment? There was no harassment. The woman was—"

"Not the woman," Combover corrected. "Mr. Holton, your previous roommate."

"What?" I said. "He seemed more than happy to be well when he checked out of here."

"Checked out?" the woman said. "Dr. Thomas, his family asked to be reassigned to a different room."

I opened my mouth, but no words came.

"Granted," the woman said, "his medical condition has improved slightly, but—"

Combover was quick to interject, "Thanks to an outstanding medical staff."

My mind reeled. *What are you doing now?!* I prayed (if shouting at God counts as prayer). *What's going on?*

By the time I rejoined the conversation, the woman was speaking: "—and it's certainly not our desire to prevent you from practicing your religious beliefs."

"Absolutely," Combover stressed.

"But when they infringe upon another or interfere with our medical treatments—"

I nodded. "Yes, I understand. And I give you my word, there will be no further incidents." I added the thought, "*ever*" for any who may be listening.

"We appreciate that, Dr. Thomas," the woman said. "But given your recent history on other matters."

"History?"

She glanced at her yellow pad. "The campus demonstrations at Western Washington University regarding your support of a sexual predator."

My jaw slacked. "Sean Fulton? Sean Fulton was no sexual predator."

She glanced to her colleague who chose to remain silent—an example I should have practiced. Returning to the pad, she continued. "Your recent termination from the university's faculty."

"I wasn't terminated, I quit."

"And of course your latest issue, instigating a prison riot."

Combover forced a chuckle. "You've been a busy man."

I closed my eyes. They were right, of course. And I had my reasons—but blaming Yeshua for them would do little to help my case.

The woman continued, "And, although it's a difficult decision—"

"Very difficult," Combover interrupted.

"—because of our shortage of rooms and the fear of further incidents—"

Combover quickly jumped in, "Mr. Holton is managing partner of Corning, Brown & Holton."

Ignoring him, she continued. "I'm afraid, you remaining at this facility would make it impossible to adequately assure the safety and care you deserve."

It took a moment to sink in. "You're . . . kicking me out?"

"Your wound seems to be healing quite nicely," she said.

"Faster than expected," Combover added.

"But this is all happening because—" I caught myself. She looked up from her pad. I simply shook my head.

She continued, "With proper home care there's no reason we cannot upgrade you to Outpatient status. You'll still come in so we can check your stitches and progress, but we've been assured you can be immediately released . . . under careful medical supervision."

"Medical supervision?"

"If you agree, Dr. Swenson will look after you during your convalescence."

"Patricia Swenson?"

"A friend of yours, is she not?"

"Yes."

They waited in silence as I tried to think.

"So . . ." the woman carefully inched us toward the goal line. "If this meets with your approval . . ."

I finally looked up and gave the slightest nod.

Combover reached into the folder he was carrying. "Is that a yes?"

"Yes."

"Excellent." He quickly pulled out a set of papers and neatly placed them on the table before me.

"If you'll read this over, initial here and here . . . and sign here, we'll have you on your way in no time."

"With best of wishes," the woman said.

"Yes," Combover agreed. "Our very best wishes."

CHAPTER
FIVE

THE GOOD NEWS was Patricia and Darlene were busy teaching at the University—i.e., they were lecturing their students instead of me—at least for today. But every silver lining has its cloud. Chip would be driving me home.

"Where's Amber?" I asked as an orderly loaded me into the wheelchair for my ride to the exit where Chip's Jeep waited.

"Oh, she's way too embarrassed, dude."

"Embarrassed?"

He motioned to the potato chips I hadn't opened from lunch. "Are you going to eat those?"

"Knock yourself out. What do you mean, embarrassed?"

Scooping up the bag, he answered, "No offense, but she never wants to be seen in public with you again." Off my look, he shrugged. "Chicks, go figure, right?" He tore open the bag and dug in. "She'll get over it."

"Get over what?"

Through the crunching he answered, "The video, dude."

"Video?"

"You've gone viral."

"I've what?"

"Check it out." Heading down the hall, he wiped the grease from his fingers, pulled out his phone, and handed it me. And there I was: On screen, half-dragged, half-carried away from the woman having a heart attack and shouting over the shrill beeping, *"Be healed! Be healed!"* It only lasted five seconds but long enough to tighten my gut. And it wasn't over. The performance repeated itself. *"Be healed! Be healed!"* Then, again. *"Be healed! Be healed!"* And again. *"Be healed! Be—"* I shoved the phone back at Chip.

"Pretty cool," he said.

"It didn't . . . that's not how it happened."

"Sure, I get it."

But of course he didn't. "Have other people seen this?" I asked.

"Like I said, it's gone viral. Big time. You're famous, dude. Check this out." He turned his phone to me to show a shorter version: no sound, just the written text, *"Be healed!"* that repeated itself in a never-ending loop of me opening my mouth and silently shouting, *"Be healed! Be healed!"*

"A meme," Chip said. "You got your very own meme."

I could only stare.

"And if we can find a way to monetize this. You know, get a sponsor. There's no telling where this could . . ."

He continued his ramblings but I no longer heard. I was too busy looking down, pretending to rub my face as we passed one staff member after another who pretended not to stare. Was I angry? You think? I had done what Yeshua wanted and this was my reward? How do you not be a bit upset when you've been betrayed by the Creator of the Universe? Then there was the minor issue of being a Guinea pig in some training program he never bothered to explain—except it involved fighting off Medes whose last king, according to Google, lived 2,500 years ago.

Somehow, we made it to Chip's Jeep. Of course he wanted to talk, but I had better things to do. Like sulk. I begged off any conversation, explaining I needed to get some sleep, which was the truth—being the village idiot is exhausting business. But, unable to endure any silence over 3.8 seconds, Chip soon treated us to his Spotify list of alt-rock-grunge-metal-whatever-you-call-it cranked up to a few decibels above *ear bleed*.

Job never had it so good.

We were halfway to the Anacortes Ferry, somewhere between Burlington and Sedro Woolley, when I suddenly found myself in a bare, heavily shadowed room. The lack of accommodations and the stench of an open sewer suggested some sort of prison. This time there were no angels or special effects. Just a young man rising from his wooden pallet. He was not exactly shocked at seeing me, but not exactly at ease either.

"Is this . . . are you another dream?" he asked.

"What? No," I said. "Are you?"

He frowned, confused. The feeling was mutual. I scanned the small room—dirt floor, walls of what looked like heavily thatched reeds, and occasional shafts of sunlight pouring through a roof that said rain wasn't a concern.

"Please," he motioned to his wooden pallet which had as many gaps as the roof.

"You see me," I said.

His frown deepened. "Are you an angel?"

I shook my head. His tattered clothes and half-starved body said I needn't ask the same.

"I'm Joseph," he offered. Looking up and down my own wardrobe, he ventured, "You're a foreigner? You were captured by Pharaoh?"

It was my turn to frown. Joseph . . . Pharaoh . . . one-star accommodations . . . "Joseph?" I ventured. "Are you the kid with the amazing technicolor dreamcoat?" (Sadly, I related more to the musical than the biblical account.)

"Um . . ." He scratched a moth-eaten beard that hadn't come into its own yet. "I did have a coat of many colors, if that's what you mean."

Close enough. "And you're here because . . . ?"

"God gave me a dream, a promise I knew was from him."

"And . . ."

"I told my brothers, but they rejected it. And not just the promise." He motioned to the room. "They rejected me."

His story felt vaguely familiar.

"And God," I asked, "what did he say about that?"

He looked away. I waited.

Finally he spoke, a quiet mumble, "He hasn't spoken to me since."

The story felt *very* familiar. Before I could press the issue, I heard a disturbance. We turned to see a much older man—stooped, thick beard, face leathered by decades of sun. He brandished a large walking stick. "Where am I?" he demanded. "What is this place?"

The kid and I traded looks.

"Sir," Joseph said, "you are in Egypt."

"Impossible," he growled. "Not again. Unless . . . is this another vision?"

Welcome to the party, I thought.

Hobbling through the room, checking it out, he grumbled, "I was outside my tents at the Oaks of Mamre when—"

"The Oaks of Mamre?" Joseph asked.

"Yes. I was having some very strong words with Jehovah when—"

"Jehovah?" Joseph interrupted again. "You know Jehovah?"

The man scowled. "You've heard of him?"

The kid could only stare.

The old-timer continued. "He said, he gave me his word that I would soon have a son."

I tried not to chuckle. "At your age?"

He turned on me. "You have spoken with my wife?"

"Your wife? No, I, uh—"

"She laughed too."

I said nothing, keeping a careful eye on his walking stick.

"Your wife," Joseph continued cautiously, his voice growing reverent. "Her name, is it . . . Sarah?"

The old man spun to him. "You *have* spoken with her!"

Joseph lowered his head, then slowly dropped to his knees.

"What are you doing?" the man demanded.

Joseph whispered in awe, "Father Abraham."

"What?" Abraham turned from Joseph to me. "Who are you!?"

Suddenly he moved in slow motion. I knew the reason and searched the room until I saw Yeshua stepping out of the shadows. "Still upset with me?" he asked.

I chose not to speak.

Motioning to the scene before us, he said, "You see the pattern, don't you?"

I frowned, trying to understand.

"Writers see patterns, that's how we designed you." When I couldn't answer, he smiled and said, "Here's another."

Suddenly the room filled with angry voices:

"Why'd you come down here?" one demanded.

"Who's watching the sheep?" another shouted.

"We know how conceited you are," the first voice accused, "how wicked your heart is. You came to gawk at Goliath, didn't you—to watch us battle the Philistines."

The voices faded and I said, "Goliath . . . as in David and Goliath?"

Yeshua nodded. "Just before David killed him. Will, the second step after belief is always doubt and rejection— particularly by those closest to you. Joseph and his brothers, David and his family, Abraham's wife—"

"And my little group?" I questioned.

"For starters."

"For starters?" He said nothing. I took advantage of the moment. "You weren't there when I prayed over that guy in the hospital. Or the woman."

"Of course I was."

"With the guy, okay, that's obvious. But why didn't you step in with the woman?"

"Why did *you*?"

"Why did I? Because . . . because, she was going to die!"

"Was she?"

I started to answer, then remembered the orderlies bursting in with the cart.

"Will, just because we give you a sword doesn't mean you wield it around like some child with a toy. It's a weapon. It requires practice."

"Practice? For what?"

"Saving the world."

"It's a little above my pay grade, don't you think?"

"If it wasn't, we'd find someone else." I scowled and he continued, "If it's any consolation, you're right on schedule."

"Schedule?

"For what we've dreamed you can be."

"You've got a dream for me?"

"Of course."

"You've had this planned?"

"You think this is all an accident?"

I wasn't sure how to respond. He saved me the trouble. "The first step was you've chosen to believe my promises."

He had me there.

"Step two—facing rejection."

"It's become a habit."

"Usually by those closest to you. The third step—well, that will come soon enough."

"Third step? How many are there?"

"Be patient. Saving the world takes time."

I blew out a breath of frustration. "Why do you always have to be so, so—"

Before I said something I'd regret (another habit of mine), I was back in the car with just Chip, his pounding music, and my ringing, bleeding ears.

CHAPTER
SIX

AMBER'S FIFTEENTH BIRTHDAY party was everything she never dreamed of—and less. Actually, that's not true. She was thrilled when Darlene caught an early ferry over and took her out for a complete makeover. To have a pedicure and manicure was terrific, but it was the flattop buzz cut that took her breath away.

Her uncle's too. (The green tinge an added bonus.)

Amber chose to have a small party. Truth is she had few friends on the island and aimed to keep them by refusing to acknowledge she was related to the crazy, old, meme guy all over the internet. So it was just Darlene, Patricia, Chip, Billie-Jean, and Siggy, who refused to leave my side lest I sneak back into heaven. I was also allowed to join them—perks of owning the establishment.

The meme not only went viral, but once the internet jockeys realized the faith healer was the same as the preacher who started prison riots and defended sexual predators . . . well, it wasn't long before I had to turn off my phone.

"Just as well," Darlene said. "Every time you try to clear up a mess—"

Patricia concluded, "—you make it worse."

It was nice to see the two finally agree on something.

Despite the mosquitoes, thick this time of summer, we opened Amber's gifts out on the deck where rippled clouds over the San Juans faded to dark pink then eggplant purple.

"What's this?" Amber asked as I handed her my gift-wrapped envelope.

"Open it," I said.

She did . . . then looked to me with the same question.

"It's a savings bond," I explained.

"A what?"

"For college. Two, five-hundred-dollar US Savings Bonds to put toward your education."

The silence was deafening. And not just Amber's.

Always helpful, Chip came to my rescue. "Or a car."

I explained, "The interest rate is 2.5 percent."

Amber stared another moment before reaching over and setting them beside another favorite—the framed photo of a Nigerian orphan Patricia would sponsor in her name. Like I said, she had better birthdays.

But Chip saved the day. Excusing himself, he returned with a bouquet of helium balloons shaped like sunflowers and tulips.

"Oh, Chip!" Amber rose and practically threw herself at him in either love or relief.

He acknowledged the affection by breathing the helium of an opened balloon and doing a pretty bad Yoda—or Wicked Witch of the East: *"Welcome, you are my pretty, yes you are."*

Amber giggled and found another excuse to hug him, throwing in a kiss so passionate even Darlene glanced away.

As they came up for air, Chip handed her another present he'd been hiding. It was a small box Amber immediately grabbed and immediately tore open. Looking inside, she practically melted. "Oh, babe . . ."

"What is it?" Patricia asked.

She pulled out a burgundy leather, gilded page, Bible.

I stared in disbelief.

"See," Chip pointed to the cover. "It's got your name printed right there on the front."

"This is sooo beautiful," she said.

"A Bible?" I asked, still trying to comprehend.

"Not just any Bible," Chip said. "Check out the front page."

Amber ran her hand over the pebbled texture before she opened the cover and gasped.

"What is it?" Darlene asked.

"The Trevor Hunter Study Bible," Chip said. "See, it's got his autograph inside and everything."

Amber looked up to him, eyes filling with tears of gratitude.

"And . . ." he proudly produced another, smaller and softer package.

She ripped it open and pulled out a skimpy pair of leotards—nowadays christened, yoga pants. "Is it . . . ?"

Chip just smiled as she unfolded them to reveal printed words along the waist band: *Jesus loves you and so do we.*

"From Jordan?" It wasn't a squeal, but close.

"And me," Chip said, pretending to sound indignant— which called for another set of hugs and lip wrangling.

As they went at it, I turned to Darlene who explained. "*Jordan* Hunter, Trevor's wife. She has her own fashion line."

Later, as the lovebirds took a moonlit stroll on the beach—at least I hoped they were strolling—I sat on the sofa as Patricia prepared to change my dressing and Darlene lay on the floor playing with Billie-Jean. We'd become quite the eclectic family. Darlene, the surrogate mother/grandmother for Amber and Billie-Jean. Chip, Amber's inseparable love (and believe me, I'd tried separation). And Patricia and me who, well who knew what we were. Certainly not boyfriend girlfriend, she made that clear— though no one else seemed to get the picture.

Of course I was attracted to her fashion model beauty, though a few extra pounds on that willowy frame wouldn't hurt. But I was also drawn to her honesty. As a missionary kid growing up in the wilds of Papua New Guinea, she never mastered irony or half-truths—skills so necessary for survival in our culture. More than a few found her lack of social skills blunt and off-putting. For me, it was not only refreshing, but when they left her feeling awkward and vulnerable, I found them endearing. What she saw, or pretended not to see, in me, I had no idea.

"I don't want to look a gift horse in the mouth," I said, "but when did this whole religious thing start with them?"

"Chip's idea, mostly," Darlene said while making goofy faces at the baby. "Probably started with this kid getting her heart healed."

"A definite miracle," Patricia said. Then to Darlene, "even by your standards."

Darlene ignored her and blew a raspberry into Billie-Jean's tummy.

Patricia turned to me. "Then there was the way you pulled through even when the doctors said it was impossible."

"Don't worry about them," Darlene said. "It's just a phase. They'll snap out of it."

Ignoring her, Patricia said, "Go ahead and take off your shirt."

I started unbuttoning it. "And their thing for this Trevor Hunter guy?"

"He seems a good man," Patricia said. "And the way he and his wife are able to reach young people for Christ, they've definitely got a gift."

Lifting Billie-Jean into the air, Darlene added, "One ol' Chipper has been trying to cash in on with that meme of yours. Writing them, calling them, emailing."

"The boy can be a pest," I said.

Darlene agreed, "*He's* got the gift."

"Are you holding in your stomach?" Patricia asked.

"What? No," I said.

"I'm a professional, Will. You don't have to try and impress me."

"Good luck with that," Darlene quipped.

"Right," I agreed, knowing that ship set sail long ago. "It's just, when I'm injured like this and I can't go to the gym, I start losing muscle tone."

Darlene threw me a look, "You go to the gym?"

"Of course." It was another lie. But being the class act Patricia was, she felt no need to correct me—particularly with so many other issues to be working on. Issues I suspect were part of the reason she allowed me to tag along with her to church. Tomorrow being no exception.

CHAPTER
SEVEN

IT WAS MY first public appearance since the prison riot and my performance at the hospital. And it wasn't bad. Truth is, after my media blunders defending Sean Fulton and his alleged sexual assaults, I'd grown used to being a public pariah. And to Patricia's credit, you could barely see her uneasiness as we walked into her church—a dimly lit warehouse full of candles and college students sipping coffee around small tables. Nevertheless, we sat at the back to avoid judgment from any of the more open-minded, woke crowd.

As usual, Patricia looked fantastic in a modest dress of printed daises and a lime green scarf. Then again, she'd look fantastic in a gunny sack. And me? After my first visit, I lost the tie and sports coat, learning to dress casually, making it clear I wasn't concerned about appearances—no matter how long I spent in front of the mirror to look it.

Several days had passed since Yeshua dropped by for a visit. Yet, in a strange way, I was seeing him more often. Sometimes in the way shafts of morning light cut through the fog and fir boughs. Or in the way Billie-Jean's tiny hands clutched my fingers. Even in the gentle hiss of the tide sliding in and out across the sand. If I couldn't enjoy a face-to-face with the author, I could at least enjoy his work.

Patricia's minister was always great. Giving up his career as an astrophysicist, Dr. Stewart's talks proved you didn't have to commit intellectual suicide to be a Christian. Today's sermon was no different. Standing before us, coffee in hand, he read a text from Ephesians:

"For our struggle is not against flesh and blood, but against the rulers, against the authorities, against the powers of this dark world and against the spiritual forces of evil in the heavenly realms."

"Heavenly realms," he said in his slight Jamaican accent. "Forgive me, but once again I must speak of these other dimensions. Not above us in the clouds, or somewhere beyond Jupiter, but here in this very room with us now. I know scientific theories come and go—and I know I speak of this often—but the latest superstring theories indicate we must be surrounded by a minimum of twenty-two dimensions." (You can take the theoretical physicist out of physics but you can't take the physics out of the theoretical physicist.)

Sadly, I soon stopped paying much attention. I was distracted by what looked like flashes of light shooting back and forth over our heads. I glanced to Patricia who, as usual was taking copious notes, then to the kids around us. No one seemed to notice. When I tried following the lights, staring at them, they faded. But when I glanced to the side, they grew more defined, like flickering flames.

As we stood for the final song, things grew even stranger. By the third or fourth line, the lights began to blossom, melding into each other. Soon the entire space above us glowed, undulating like an interior Aurora Borealis. It seemed to affect our worship too, deepening it, making it more real. But it wasn't just *our* worship. I began hearing other voices. Hundreds of them. Like a giant choir, their notes weaving in and out of each other in intricate harmonies. I'd heard this music once before. In heaven . . . when its light washed through me with its indescribable peace. For a moment I was back there, the music seeping into my soul, bringing tears of joy.

It wasn't until I felt Patricia touch my arm, "Will? Will, are you alright?" that I was back in the coffeehouse.

I looked around, getting my bearings. "Yeah," I wiped my eyes. "I'm, uh . . . I'm fine."

Of course, Patricia knew better, but with the students surrounding us she had the good sense not to pursue. We joined them and headed out the exit. That's when I caught the whiff of sulfur, a stench like rotten eggs. And it's when I saw the shadows—dirty smudges hovering nearby, but refusing to come too close.

"What are you looking at?" There was no missing the concern in Patricia's voice.

Before I could answer, there was the squeal of brakes and a dull, sickening *thump*—followed by the scream of students. We spun around to see a white Mercedes, not twenty feet away, sitting at an angle in the street. In front of it lay a body, unmoving. Patricia immediately broke into action, pushing her way through the crowd. He was a young man, probably from the church. He wore a denim shirt with khaki shorts. His left leg was impossibly twisted, like a broken doll's. Not far away a pair of mirrored sunglasses lay on the pavement.

I moved to follow as Patricia dropped to her knees, pressed an ear to his mouth, felt his neck for a pulse. Only then did I notice the blood pumping out of his left thigh.

Spotting me, she yelled, "Give me your hand!"

"What?"

She motioned for me to join her. I kneeled and she grabbed my wrist with one hand, while ripping off her scarf with the other. She shoved the scarf into my hand and pulled it to the spurting hole in the boy's leg. Pushing it into the wound, she yelled, "Hold it there!" She dragged my other hand to join it. "As hard as you can!"

I did my best, though blood poured from the scarf, running between my fingers.

Patricia returned to the boy's head, adjusting it before opening his mouth and placing hers over it. Only then did I notice someone else kneeling beside us. The gymnast.

There was no urgency in his face, no concern. He simply looked at me and shook his head.

"What?" I cried. "He's not going to make it?"

Patricia heard but ignored me as she took another breath and blew it into the boy's mouth.

Again the gymnast shook his head.

"What?" I repeated.

He motioned me to move my hands, directing them to the kid's chest.

I frowned, not understanding.

He motioned again.

"No," I said, "*this* is where he's bleeding."

"Yes," Patricia said, "the femoral artery. Don't let up!"

The gymnast continued shaking his head, motioning to the chest.

I looked down at my hands, at the scarf soaked in blood. Strangely no more of it was flowing through my fingers.

Again the gymnast motioned to the chest.

I turned to Patricia and shouted, "I think the bleeding has slowed."

She shook her head. "Keep up the pressure!"

"But—"

"Don't stop!"

Of course, Patricia knew best. But the gymnast was insistent. I hesitated, looked back to him. He just kept motioning to the chest. Slowly, ever so slightly, I removed some of the pressure. There was still no blood. I pulled back one hand to sneak a peek. The bleeding had stopped. As inconspicuously as possible, I slipped that hand from his leg and up to the chest where the gymnast indicated. Only then did I notice how hot both of my hands felt.

"What are you doing?" Patricia shouted. "Keep the pressure! He'll bleed out!"

I nodded and started to return my hand. But the gymnast shook his head, not only insisting I keep it on the chest, but motioning me to remove my other hand from the leg to join it. Against my better judgment and in spite of Patricia's expertise, I eased the other hand from the wound and set it beside the one on his chest. By now both hands felt as if they were on fire.

"Will!"

Before I could explain, the student convulsed. His entire body jerked, just once . . . before he opened his eyes.

Patricia pulled back confused—then immediately moved to the leg I had deserted. But the bleeding had stopped. She pulled away the scarf. The wound was sealed shut.

The student began struggling to sit up.

"No, no!" she shouted. "Stay down! Don't move!"

But he refused to listen, working even harder to rise. I removed my hands and watched. Only when he succeeded and sat up, did I notice the crowd surrounding us, the cell phones out and recording.

"Hey, man!" someone shouted. "You okay?"

The kid stared up at the crowd, stunned.

"Are you alright?" another asked.

Finally, he spoke. "I saw him."

"Who?" the first asked.

He swallowed. "God."

The group murmured.

He turned to me, his eyes widening. "And *you*! You were there! He asked you to bring me back to life!"

The murmurs grew louder. "Praise God," someone whispered. Others joined in. "It's a miracle. Praise God! It's a miracle. It's a miracle!!"

I turned to Patricia as she finished checking his leg. When she looked back to me, her face was filled with astonishment . . . and fear.

CHAPTER
EIGHT

"I KEEP COMING BACK to the same question," Patricia said as she picked at her gluten-free, fat-free, and I suppose taste-free muffin. It had been an hour since the police and EMS arrived at the accident and took charge. Now we were at some hole-in-the-wall restaurant a few blocks away trying to process. "I think the world of you, Will, you know that." (I didn't but I appreciated the intel.) "But why with your . . . less than stellar history, why would He choose you?"

I nodded, but not just over the accident. Truth is, I'd been asking the same question ever since Yeshua started his unannounced visits last Christmas. Still, I figured right now wasn't the time to bring those up.

"I have seen healings in the mission field. But by devout men and women of God, not by, by . . ." She chose not to finish the sentence and I wasn't disappointed. She continued, "And I've also seen counterfeits."

"Counterfeits?"

"Scripture says Satan can appear to a person as an angel of light."

I nodded, not exactly sure where I fit in that scenario.

"I just need time to pray," she said. "Maybe do a little fasting."

"Before . . . ?"

"I think we need a little time off."

And so, after walking her to her car and saying our goodbyes, I was on my own—again. What's the old saying? Christians are the only ones who shoot their wounded? Not that I was resentful. At least not toward Patricia.

It wasn't until I was back on the island and driving home that I heard the air conditioning turned to high and saw Yeshua in the passenger seat, adjusting the vent.

"You don't mind, do you?" he asked.

"Knock yourself out."

He sat back in the seat. "You angry?"

I took a deep breath and tried my best to be an adult. "Just . . . confused."

"And angry." (It's tough lying to the God who "searches every heart.") "So . . ." He waited for me to begin. And waited. And waited some more.

"Alright," I finally said. "First of all, I don't understand about that kid. Why him and not the woman at the hospital?"

"At the hospital you acted on your own. Remember what I said about a sword in the hands of a child? You wanted to do your will, you never bothered to ask me mine."

"Okay, fine. But how do I know it? How do I know the difference between your will and mine?"

"The closer we grow, the more you'll know it."

"And until then?"

"You have your Bible."

"I don't remember reading anything about middle-aged ladies in hospitals and dead college kids." I immediately regretted my snarkiness.

"I forgive you," he said. I bit my tongue. He continued, "Knowing my will comes down to hearing my voice."

"And how do I do that, if you're not always here?"

"But I am."

"You know what I mean. How do I hear your voice without this, this . . ."

Yeshua motioned to himself, "Audio visual aide?"

"Exactly."

"You've been seeing my handiwork in nature, haven't you?"

"That counts?"

"Appreciating masterpieces can help appreciate the artist."

I looked out the window—the sun strobing through a grove of passing cedars, the light highlighting their textured bark.

"See what I mean?"

"Okay," I said.

"Solitude is also important."

"Solitude? You mean like—" I came to a stop. "Is that why Patricia is cutting me off?"

He gave no answer and looked out the window. Moments passed before he continued. "This is important too. Tell me, what were you doing just before the accident, inside the church?"

"Besides seeing some very strange creatures, which I'm guessing are more of your friends."

He smiled. "With this new seeing of yours comes new territory. But tell me, what were you doing?"

"We were singing."

"Worshipping," he corrected. "You were aligning your heart with the rest of my creation."

I nodded, slowly coming to the realization. "And back at the hospital with that woman—I did none of that."

He sighed quietly. "So many good people rely on their strength to accomplish my will."

"And that's wrong?"

"Not always wrong, but always worthless . . . if they don't wait to hear my will."

"Not everyone can pop into a church for downloads."

"But you *are* the church, Will." I turned to him and he continued. "Your body is my Spirit's temple. Strength is good but the key to finding my will is to enter your Holy of Holies, to commune with me."

"No offense, but that sounds just a little New Ageish."

"Remember, Satan creates nothing new. The parasite can only twist my truth into his perversion."

It was starting to make sense, but he knew I had more on my mind.

"Go ahead," he said. "Ask."

I took a breath and began. "When the kid on the street, when he woke up, he said he saw me in heaven."

"That's right."

"But . . . how?"

"Your pastor friend quoted a verse from Paul's letter to the Ephesians. Mind listening to another?"

"Please."

He lifted his head, closed his eyes, and quoted, *"And God raised us up with Christ and seated us with him in the heavenly realms."*

"In the future," I said. "Later, when I'm dead."

"You're an English prof. *'Raised'. . . 'seated.'* Seems those verbs are past not future tense."

"But how's that possible—being in two places at the same time?"

He smiled. "Quantum physics may not be your strong suit." Then, growing more serious, he said. "Your greatest struggle, the one I keep mentioning, is that you don't know your identity. Like Gideon, you refuse to understand who you are."

"You keep saying that."

"And you keep forgetting it. Did I mention, you'll also be judging angels?"

I snorted and shook my head.

"What?" he said.

"Maybe someday, but for now, let's face it, I'm a train wreck. For now, I'm just some wretched sinner lucky to even be—"

"Stop it!" The outburst shocked me into silence. "You're trivializing my sacrifice again." He wasn't shouting, at least not with his voice. "You still believe the accuser's lies. You still believe my agony and death were insufficient." He took a moment to gather his composure. "You're a new creature, Will. You have to get that in your head and get on the *other* side of the cross. Yes, you *were* wretched. Yes, you *were* vile. Even your best works were like menstrual rags."

That's a bit graphic, I thought.

Look it up, he thought back, then continued speaking, "But when I climbed up on that cross to be tortured to death, it was for you. So you are clean. So you're a brand-new creature."

"But . . ." I spoke softly, not to rile him further. "I still sin. I keep messing up."

"And I keep forgiving—as quickly as you confess. So stop believing the accuser's lie. Stop crawling back to the wrong side of the cross, thinking you're some dead, rotten corpse."

"But you talk about humility."

"That's not humility. That's the parasite twisting my truth to cripple and hobble you. You're a new creature, Will Thomas. You have my Spirit. My power. My authority. Act like it."

It was a lot to take in. "It's just . . . I'm sorry for always arguing—"

"Seeking truth is not arguing."

"Okay. But it's just . . ."

"Go ahead."

"I see religious people like you're talking about all the time. They strut around with all the answers, acting like they're God's gift to humanity."

"They *are* my gift."

"Strutting around like rock stars?"

"No. Not rock stars. Servants. Like me. Like you. Our gift to the world is not strutting. Our gift is washing feet."

CHAPTER
NINE

MY HEAD STILL reeled. I turned onto the driveway, gravel popping under my tires, when I slammed on the brakes and slid to a stop. In front of me stood the angel guard from my hospital room. He glanced to his left, then to his right before giving a nod. I heard a grating sound, like a giant iron gate sliding open. I saw nothing but when it stopped, he stepped aside, bowed his head and motioned for me to enter. To say I was unnerved was an understatement. Looking every direction, I slowly inched forward. As I passed, he dissolved into the afternoon sun and shadow.

But I had little time to marvel. Old man Carothers's pickup was parked up ahead. As usual Chip had taken my spot with his Jeep which left me no choice but to pull into the weeds and park so Carothers could exit—and the sooner the better. It's not that he was a crank, he was just . . . well alright, he was a crank and then some.

With nerves still on edge and more than a little suspicious, I stepped from my car and walked over to join him.

He stood by my kitchen door leaning on his walker. Janny, his tall, twenty-something granddaughter, slouched beside him. She was a sweet church kid (I forget which brand) who, after his recent fall, was elected to be his caregiver. We all have our crosses to bear.

Given my afternoon, I greeted him as pleasantly as possible. "Hey, there."

He answered with equal enthusiasm. "Janny here saw you on the innertube."

I gave her a look but she knew better than to correct him. "If you're talking about that hospital thing," I said, "it was all just a big—"

"I'm not talkin' no hospital. I'm talkin' about that college kid. This morning."

I looked back to Janny. Over black, stringy hair, she suddenly wore a pair of what looked like sound-dampening ear muffs, the type they wear on aircraft carriers or on shooting ranges. They were only there a moment then, like the angel, disappeared. I blinked, suspecting they had something to do with her being born almost entirely deaf— not a bad gift when it came to dealing with Carothers.

Speaking in her loud, carefully enunciated voice, she asked. "Is he okay now?"

I nodded. "As far as I can tell."

She stole a glance to Carothers then said, "All you did was pray for him and he was healed, right? All you did—"

"Bull pucky," the old man snorted.

"Grandpa," she said, "God can do that sort of thing."

"I'm not interested in your religious crap." He nodded to his right leg. "I want to know if you can fix this thing."

I looked down and was startled to see the shaft of a shimmering, black arrow lodged in his knee. But, like the angel, like Janny's earwear, it quickly dissolved. "So," I cleared my throat. "No better?"

"Does it look better? So can you do something or not?"

I glanced back to Janny who looked down. "I'm sorry," she said, "We really didn't mean to bother you. I just thought, *we* just thought. I mean if you could heal him and he could see God at work, maybe he . . ." She let the thought fade but we both read between its lines. Healing Carothers's leg would not only fix his body but probably do something for his soul.

"So?" he repeated.

I felt my hands growing warm just as they had with the student. If I needed a sign, this was it. I looked down at them and then up into his face, his bushy brows furrowed in a scowl. Yeshua could reach anybody—me being a prime example. I turned to Janny, saw the hope in her face. I swallowed, then stepped to Carothers. I set my hand on his flannel shirt hanging loosely over his boney shoulders. He flinched but did not move. Janny joined us, taking a safer approach, touching me as I touched him. I closed my eyes and began to pray—not my televangelist imper-sonation at the hospital but my halting, self-conscious version—trusting Yeshua's promise that the Holy Spirit would translate it into something coherent:

"God . . . would you, you know, if it's not too much trouble . . . we could sure use a healing here, if that's okay. Uh . . . Amen." I opened my eyes, pulled back my hand, and waited.

We all waited.

Finally Janny asked, "How do you feel, Grandpa?"

He moved his leg and winced. "Bad as always."

Janny and I traded looks. He moved it again, this time adding a colorful oath.

"You have to have faith, Grandpa."

"Faith?" He moved it more and swore more. "That college kid didn't have no faith. He was out cold."

I reached back to him. "Here, let me try again. Let me—"

"No," he pushed away my hand. "You done enough." Then to Janny. "It's time for lunch."

"Grandpa—"

"We tried your thing and it didn't work. Let's go."

"Gran—"

"Now!"

She hesitated then silently agreed. As they passed, she mouthed a *thank you*. I nodded and watched them amble toward his pickup. I should have said something, but what? "God hates grumps?" "Win a few, lose a few?" "Better luck next time?"

Fortunately, Chip saved me the effort. He opened the kitchen screen door and, speaking into his phone, stepped out to join me. "That's right," he said, "3425 McElroy Road. Little cottage overlooking the water, can't miss it." I gave him a questioning look. He gave me a thumbs-up and continued. "That's right, four o'clock. Wonderful. God bless you. Jesus loves you and so do we."

"Who was that?" I asked as he disconnected.

"Your four o'clock."

"My four—"

"Dr. Thomas!" We turned to Janny and Carothers who had stopped at his pickup. She removed a hand from her left ear and was covering her right. "Dr. Thomas! I can hear!" She giggled and uncovered her right. "I can hear! Everything!"

I stared, amazed, as she continued laughing, checking and rechecking her ears—until my attention was drawn to a vehicle I did not recognize; a white SUV turned onto the driveway and was coming down to join us.

I looked to Chip who grinned. "Your three thirty." He flipped back his hair. "Good news travels fast."

CHAPTER
TEN

MY NEXT TWO "appointments"—that's what Chip called them—were both from our island: a veteran whose left side of his face was crinkled in scar tissue; and some kid's dead hamster. My batting average with them was identical to old man Carothers. Both said they understood, but it was the little boy's questions, between tears—"Why won't he heal him? Why doesn't God like me?"—that gnawed at me. Which is why I ordered Chip to cancel any other meetings. Sadly, it didn't stop him and Amber from working Facebook, Instagram, and starting a GoFundMe page.

"A workman is worth his wages," Chip explained. "Just like Trevor says."

"Trevor . . ."

"Trevor Hunter. And once we start asking for donations, you know, get a not-for-profit 501C going, our financial worries are over."

I wasn't fond of Chip's use of the word *our*. Nor was I thrilled continuing to hear about the great Trevor Hunter.

Sadly, my affection didn't increase when they sat me down that night to watch his show. And "show" was exactly what it was.

To be fair, it was like any other talk show—big-time celebrity guests I'd never heard of, good band, and a witty, late thirties host behind a modern, steel and glass desk. In Trevor's case, the host had a great tan, thick hair falling into his face Elvis stye, and great chiseled features (which I tried not to hold against him). Nor did I begrudge his cohost, a gorgeous red-haired beauty with all the right parts in all the right places being his wife. And yes, they were saying all the right things: "God is awesome" . . . "He's on your side" . . . "Even if you're a major loser, Jesus loves you and so do we."

Despite a dress whose neckline left no doubt about her physical attributes, and his narrow-leg jeans and white T-shirt (cut to prove he had a demanding personal trainer), the couple was what the kids call "authentic." More than anything, I was impressed with how they held Chip's and Amber's ADD attention without being gimmicky—just honest and, here's the word again, "authentic."

But it was the call for money at the end that left me cold. Not the call, but the method:

"Yeah, I get that money's tough," he said. "Me and Jordan, we hit Walmart yesterday, just the basics and boy did *we* get hit, right babe?

"You've got that right," his wife said.

"But I also know God only gives to us when we give to others. Or as the Big Man says, *'Give and it will be given to you pressed down, shaken together and running over.'*" Turning to the band leader he called, "You ever read that, Chaz?"

From his keyboard the leader shook his head, "Crazy."

"Yeah," Trevor said. "Now if you don't want 'running over,' that's cool, God still loves you; he loves everyone, right? But if you want more, I mean lots more—well, I didn't make that promise, he did. And here's the best thing; you don't have to have the money to do it. He's not going to deprive you if you're hitting hard times. It's the widow's mite, guys. If you don't have it, go ahead and sow it anyway." He pulled out a credit card and grinned. "That's what this little baby is all about." He continued, "Seriously, what better way to pay off your card than sowing back into it by faith—'cause we all know it's impossible to please God without faith. Right, babe?"

Jordan nodded. "That's right, Trev."

"So, if you got the faith, do a little sowing. Or a lot. Plant that seed in the ground and watch it grow ten, twenty, a hundredfold. *Pressed down, shaken together and running over.* I tell you, it doesn't get any better than that. You got my word on it. Better yet, you got his."

The band began playing as he thanked everyone and the credits rolled—but not before announcing some sort of revival they'd be kicking off in Las Vegas.

Amber turned to me and grinned, "So what do you think, Uncle Will?"

"I, um . . ."

"Pretty cool, isn't he?" Chip said.

"You listen to him a lot?"

"Every Friday night," Amber said.

"Almost," Chip corrected then held up Amber's Bible. "When we're not reading his Word on our own."

I nodded, rattled off something positive that I don't remember, and said I needed to hit the beach.

"Great." Chip rose. "I'll come with."

"Uh, maybe next time," I lied, then continued. "It's been a hectic day; I just need to clear my head a bit."

"And pray," Amber said.

"Right. And pray."

After mentioning to Chip it was getting late, I grabbed my coat at the back kitchen door. I called to Siggy, who went into his usual leaping, tail-chasing frenzy, and we stepped out into the thick fog. Traipsing the path around the house, we headed down the wet, wooden steps to the beach.

I loved the beach at night. The solitude. With the tide out, the silence was complete, save a distant moaning foghorn. And when we were socked in like this, the stillness was even greater, a gray cocoon muffling everything but my breathing and the soft crunch of sand under foot.

"Busy day?"

I gave a start and turned to see Yeshua strolling beside me. Same sandals. Same robe. But with a thick brown shawl over his shoulders to ward off the heavy mist.

I sighed. "Sometimes it's hard to keep up with you."

"When you're not complaining about my moving too slow?"

I gave a reluctant nod. Hard to argue with someone who knows you better than you know yourself. "What about this Trevor guy Amber and Chip are so crazy about?" I asked. "Is he for real?"

"*You will know them by their fruits,*" he quoted.

"But—"

"I know," he sighed.

"Begging for money and betting on you like you're some race horse."

"And he's the cosmic bookie?"

"Well, yeah." I shook my head. "Definitely not my style."

"I'm curious, Will. How many lives has your style changed?"

"How many lives has . . . ? I'm not . . . I mean—" I came to a stop, realizing his point.

Yeshua continued, not harsh but matter-of-fact. "I imagine he'd rather reach your niece and the tens of thousands like her with his style, than the ones you haven't reached with yours."

Even in the stillness I'm sure he heard me wince.

"Not to worry though," he said. "That's all about to change."

Great, I thought, *here it comes*.

"Only if you want it to," he said.

Free will. It was always about free will. I paused. He waited. Finally, I nodded. "Okay, hit me."

"Good," he said softly, then began. "For starters, you've both entered training."

"Training?"

"You and Trevor, you've both completed the first steps."

"Which are . . . remind me again?"

"One: You accepted my promise. Two: You've been ridiculed for it."

I nodded. "Patricia, Darlene, everyone hating me because of Sean."

"And the list will grow."

"Wonderful," I sighed. "What about this Trevor fellow? Who's ridiculed him?"

Yeshua looked at me, cocking his head.

"Me?"

"Among others." He continued, "You've both completed the first two steps. Now you're in the middle of the third: Trying to fulfill my promises your way."

"The woman at the hospital," I said. "And Carothers. And the army vet."

"And the boy with the hamster."

"Right," I chuckled, "the kid with the dead hamster."

"Who in nine years, six weeks and three days will hang himself."

I slowed to a stop. "Not because of me?"

"He'll feel deserted. That no one cares. Not even me."

"Because I couldn't heal his pet?"

"It's wheels within wheels, Will. Connections you'll never understand."

"I . . . didn't know." I looked to him. "But you did."

"A sad perk of omniscience."

I knew it wasn't entirely my fault but I stared hard at the sand . . . until I felt his hand on my shoulder and we resumed walking. "You and Trevor are in good company. You're not my only friends who've tried fulfilling my words their way."

Before I could respond, the beach shook with an explosion. I turned to see the night sky flicker with light. It was followed by a loud overhead scream and a pounding flash a dozen yards behind us. Yeshua quickly pulled me down to dry grass as tracer bullets streaked to our left. Another flash and explosion followed. Up ahead a pair of army tanks rumbled toward us.

"Where are we?" I shouted. "What's going on?"

"The Arab Israeli War!"

"Which one?"

"Exactly." Another rocket screamed overhead. "Jews and Arabs are both descendants of Abraham. The Jews from Isaac, son of Abraham's wife. The Arabs, from Ishmael, son of his wife's servant."

Another flash and thundering explosion.

"You're not going to get all political on me?" I shouted.

"Since when have you known me to get political?"

He had a point.

"Politics only address the symptom." He continued, "I made the promise to Abraham and Sarah. But thinking he'd make it happen his way, Abraham first slept with Sarah's servant. The descendants of those two have been at odds ever since."

I looked at the tanks which were much closer, lit by another flying rocket. "Are you saying that's the cause of this whole Middle East mess?"

"If Abraham had waited for me to fulfill my promise my way—"

Suddenly, we were back in silence. But not the silence of the beach. As my eyes adjusted to the dim light, I saw we were in a cave. Not far away a second Yeshua sat on a boulder—gaunt, sunburned, emaciated. Across from him, sitting on another boulder, was . . . me! Another me. The one who offered Yeshua a stone from the cave's floor. The one who suggested he turn it into bread.

"Remember when I was tested in the wilderness?" the Yeshua beside me asked.

Unable to take my eyes from the scene, I whispered, "How could I forget?"

"What would have happened if I tried fulfilling the Father's promise Satan's way—if I'd turned that stone to bread?"

I was too embarrassed to answer.

"What would have happened if I'd chosen the sensible, easier route of ruling the world the devil's way, instead of God's longer and more painful way of the cross?"

"I'd be—we'd all be . . ."

"Exactly.

I nodded. But he wasn't quite finished.

Suddenly we were in bright daylight, standing at the threshold of a first-century home. A young peasant was being dragged out, none too gently, by two other men. Inside, a woman clutching a crying baby, screamed, "Don't take him. No!" She turned to a third man who stood watching. "Have mercy! Saul, please, I beg you!"

I turned to Yeshua, "Saul?"

"Soon to be Paul."

"The apostle?"

"Certain he was doing God's work by arresting Christians."

"Please . . ." the woman dropped to her knees, "I beg you."

I watched, repeating, "Doing God's work, but his way."

"Until he had a little 'come to me' moment."

Once again, I nodded.

"And it doesn't stop there. Sadly, it's been the cause of more than one atrocity—the Crusades, the Inquisition, witch hunts."

"All done in your name."

"And people think using my name in vain is simply swearing. It's so much more." Sadly, he repeated, "So much more."

"But—" I turned to him and we were back on the beach. After getting my bearings I continued, "knowing the difference between your way and my way, that's the trick."

"No. We talked about that before. Be still. Listen to my heart, not your head. All you have to do is obey. No matter how small the step, how foolish it seems, obedience is the key. I'll take care of the rest."

"Obedience," I repeated.

"The fourth step you're about to take."

Before I could reply, my cell phone played Darth Vader's theme from *Star Wars*. Amber's ring. I looked to Yeshua who nodded for me to pick up. I pulled the phone from my pocket but barely got it to my ear before I heard Amber's voice. "Uncle Will! Uncle Will!"

"What's wrong now?" I asked.

"Guess who's on the phone with Chip? Trevor Hunter! His people! They saw Chip's post on Instagram, you healing that guy!"

"They saw—" I turned to Yeshua who was already dissolving into the fog. "What do they want?" I asked. "Why'd they call?"

"They want you to fly down to Los Angeles. They want you to be on his show!"

PART TWO

CHAPTER
ELEVEN

I'D BE A bigger fan of flying if it didn't involve climbing into a narrow, metal tube with 176 total strangers, careening seven miles over the earth at 600 mph, and thinking I'd somehow survive. (And people say trusting God takes faith.) But I wasn't completely on my own. Utilizing his pre–San Quinton, con artist skills, Chip not only talked Trevor's ministry into picking up my travel expenses but, since he was my "associate," his expenses as well.

Now, sitting beside me, he devoured a pocket New Testament like a starving man, often asking questions I'd barely considered myself, let alone could answer. And, although I hated to admit it, from time to time there were moments like these, where I didn't entirely find him irritating. Fortunately, they were few and far between.

Patricia's and Darlene's reactions to the invite were different from Chip's and Amber's. Patricia, because she was certain I wasn't ready for primetime representation of God, and Darlene because she thought I was aiding and abetting a snake oil salesman. I found it hard to disagree on either account. But obedience was obedience. And, like it or not, this one had God's fingerprints (and irony) all over it.

LAX was the madhouse I expected. Every brand and persuasion of humanity elbow to elbow, each lost in their own cell phone or ear-bud reality. It wasn't until we entered baggage claim when I heard, "Dr. Thomas! Dr. Thomas!" I turned to see a young man, late twenties, in beard and dark, shoulder-length hair. He wore cargo pants, Hawaiian shirt, and flip-flops. "Will Thomas?"

I nodded.

"Puget Healy." He gave me a knuckle bump. "You can call me Pug."

Before I answered, Chip stepped in. "And I'm Chip Brunswick, Dr. Thomas's associate. You can call me Chip."

"Cool," Pug said. "Listen, Trev sends his apologies. He wanted to meet you in person but something came up."

"In person?" I said. "I really didn't expect him to—"

"One of the cleaning ladies, her kid got hurt in soccer. He's at the ER praying with them, but he'll meet you at the house. He hopes you understand."

I did and I didn't. A busy celebrity like "Trev" taking time to pray over a staff's kid? Not exactly the strutting rooster I'd created in my head. Maybe Yeshua was right, maybe I had misjudged him.

After wrestling multiple suitcases from the luggage carousel (Amber helped me pack), Pug signaled a porter and said, "He'll take care of these."

"It's okay." I turned to Chip. "My associate can use the exercise."

"No worries," Pug said. "Another car is on its way to pick them up."

"Another car?"

"Come on."

We followed him onto a shuttle that took us to a sprawling parking lot. From there it was a short walk to . . .

"An Alfa Romeo?" Chip said as we approached the gleaming, forest green sports car.

"Alfa Romeo Giulia Quadrifoglio," Pug corrected. "Eight speed complete with Race Mode, 0-60 in 3.8 seconds."

I might have heard Chip gulp.

"The Lamborghini is in the shop."

Chip turned to me with a huge smile.

We took the 101 North heading to Malibu, Trevor's home and headquarters. Pug proved to be a seasoned LA driver—zipping in and out between cars as if they were standing still—which, more often than not, they were. Having been to heaven once already, I wasn't as concerned about the possible outcome as I might have been. However, it was unnerving to see my gymnast friend, (alright, I'll call him the Holy Spirit) sitting up on the sunroof, legs crossed, enjoying the wind blowing through his hair. Even more unsettling was his rapping on the glass when Pug started taking the exit for the Santa Monica Freeway to Malibu.

I stole a look to Pug who, of course, heard nothing. Then back up to the Spirit who was motioning for us to stay on the 101. I thought of ignoring him, but knowing how successful that proved in the past, I turned back to Pug. "Uh, listen," I said. "If you don't mind, can we stay on this freeway a bit longer?"

"We gotta take the Santa Monica to get to Malibu," he said.

"Right. I just, uh . . ." With no help from above (literally), I improvised. "Didn't I see a UCLA sign back there?"

"Yeah . . ." Then, catching on, Pug said, "That's right, you're a college prof."

"Was," Chip corrected.

Pug flashed me a grin. "Want to check out the competition, huh? Maybe fill out a job app?"

"Okay . . ."

"Cool. That's where Trev is now; at their hospital with Maria's kid."

"Ahh," I said, starting to get a clue.

"Great idea. Let's meet him there. The dude's connected; I bet he could put in a good word for you. Cool?"

"Right," I said, glancing up at the sunroof just in time to see the Spirit turn to a bird and fly away. "Cool."

CHAPTER
TWELVE

IT ONLY TOOK one call to find the hospital room Trevor was visiting—and to alert his team they'd be having company.

"Team?" I asked Pug.

"Trev likes hanging with his videographer."

I caught Chip nodding to me and silently mouthing the word, *cool*.

"Videographer?"

"Social media," he said. "How cool it'll be to see the two of you together: Miracle Man and . . . hey, wait a minute—if the kid's sick, how awesome if you did your healing thing."

"Healing thing?"

"And get some B-roll stuff while we're at it."

"B-roll?"

My associate quickly explained. "Extra footage. Something to cut away to when you're on the show."

"Exactly," Pug said.

"Um . . ." There was no missing the hesitancy in my voice.

"I know, I know," Pug grinned. "As the Spirit leads, right?"

If he only knew.

We crossed the plaza from the parking lot and took an elevator to the third floor. Once the doors hissed open, we turned left and headed down a long, sun-lit hallway. Chip's new sneakers, the ones he'd gone in debt over for the occasion, squeaked loudly on the polished floor as I silently prayed, *What am I supposed to do now?*

Of course there was no answer.

As we approached the nurse's station, Chip continued to grill Pug on the joys of SoCal life, particularly surfing—which Pug, who hit the waves nearly every day, was only too happy to share—which Chip, the perpetual opportunist, was only too happy to exploit.

"So maybe you could show me?" he asked.

"I'm kinda busy, little dude," Pug said. "But we'll find somebody. Maybe Trev's daughter. She's hot."

"Yeah?"

"Smokin'."

"Cool," Chip chirped. Glancing at me, he cleared his throat and added, "We'll have to see, though. My schedule is pretty full."

"Cool."

We reached the nurse's station. I wasn't entirely surprised to see the white dove I had seen fly from the sunroof.
He was perched on the counter preening his feathers, waiting. Pug asked which room Trevor Hunter was in. Not the
patient, but Trevor Hunter. The nurse, a young woman,
late twenties, knew exactly who he meant and directed
us to the right and down the hall. Pug thanked her and
headed right. The dove fluttered into the air and flew left.
Since Chip and Pug were lost in discussing the difference
between hollow and peaky waves, I followed to the left.

Where are we going now? I thought. But even as I
prayed, I remembered God never telling Abraham where
he was going until he got there. I sighed. No reason he'd
change his MO for me.

We reached a stairway. I opened the door and followed
the dove up two flights until we arrived at the maternity
floor. Pushing open the door, I saw the nurse's station on
one side of the hallway, the nursery with its glass wall on
the other. But this was no ordinary nursery. Or maybe it
was. Because at the head of each of the fourteen bassinets
stood a soldier. Alert and on guard. In many ways they
reminded me of the ones I had seen outside my own hospital window.

At the nurse's station a thin, neurotic woman with
nervous hands was busy filing papers. She never bothered
to look up. Across from her, at the nursery's closed door,
stood another familiar figure; the warrior with the jagged

scar down his face. As we approached, a heavy-set nurse with oversized glasses opened the door and stepped out. She called to the nervous nurse who rose from her station and crossed the hall, apparently to trade places. Amazingly, neither of them saw us.

Nurse Neurotic entered the nursery. The warrior motioned me to follow. I balked. He frowned. The dove flew past us and inside. I continued to hesitate. The warrior's frown knitted into a deep scowl—not angry, but not exactly happy. The other soldiers looked up. I fidgeted. Finally, and impatiently, the warrior simply cleared his throat. It was an exploding boom that settled into deafening thunder. Point made. With ears still ringing, I slipped in just before the door closed. Standing there, heart beating, I searched for an excuse to use should the nurse turn around and bust me. But she never turned. She moved among the bassinets, stopping once or twice to check an infant, but she never turned.

The dove perched on a bassinet across the room. I had a growing list of excuses to stay by the door. But there was my warrior buddy and all his pals . . . watching, waiting. Finally, sucking it up, I started forward. Only then did I notice my hands growing hot.

The room was peaceful, smelling of baby powder and warm, fresh linen. Full disclosure here: Before Billie-Jean, I was never much of a baby fan—seeing them as all demand at one end and no responsibility at the other. But gazing down at them, some with blue ribbons around their bassinets, others with pink—well, what I once described as alien-looking life-forms now appeared as cute and, dare I admit it, adorable.

When I finally joined the dove and looked down, I saw a baby boy. But, unlike the others, his face was blue. And he wasn't moving. Alarmed, I looked back to the dove. He cooed softly and ruffled his feathers. I didn't know what he meant. (Or pretended I didn't.) I turned to the nurse, her back still to me. The dove continued to wait, quietly preening himself. My hands grew hotter. A trickle of sweat inched down my temple.

Suddenly, and in a stroke of genius, I called, "Nurse? Excuse me, this baby . . . Nurse?"

But she didn't turn, apparently not hearing.

"This baby needs help."

Still no response.

I looked to the baby, then to the dove who simply cocked his head at me. Finally, with no other alternative, though I guess I always have one, I stretched down my hands and rested them on the child's chest. He gasped, took a breath, and broke into an ear-shattering scream.

That's when the nurse heard.

Spinning around, eyes widening, she cried, "What are you doing in here! What are you doing to that child?"

Before I could explain, she turned to the nurse's station and through the window shouted, "Security! CALL SECURITY!"

CHAPTER

THIRTEEN

"SO, HOW MUCH?" Chip asked as we climbed out of Pug's Alfa Romeo and stood before a sprawling castle, complete with a towering turret, overlooking the Pacific. Next to it sat the headquarters/studio—a sleek, low-lying structure of glass and steel. "I mean the house, the headquarters, everything" he said. "How much, all in?"

Pug laughed. "No idea."

"None?" Chip asked.

"It's not a deal," Pug said as we started across the cobblestone driveway to the house.

"Not a deal?" Chip asked. "Either way, I suppose business must be good, right?"

Pug agreed. "There's a whole world out there that needs God, bro."

"Amen," Chip said, flipping back his hair and turning to me. I shaded my eyes from the glare off the ocean to see him grinning.

There was good news and there was bad. The good? When the hospital learned I was part of Trevor Hunter's "entourage," they chose to forgo any charges. The fact I'd help save the baby's life didn't hurt. And the bad? Chalk that up to Trevor's social media team. Even though I refused to go on camera or stick around to meet and pose with Trevor, the nurses couldn't wait to be interviewed for their fifteen seconds of fame. The camera guy also managed to grab a shot from the window of me racing across the plaza to the parking lot—which I'm told only increased interest in the, "Mysterious Miracle Man."

Back at the castle, we entered through a tall, wooden plank door. The floor of the entry hall, in fact of the entire structure, consisted of giant slabs of black slate, textured just enough to remind us we were still in medieval times. On either side were two massive staircases sweeping up to the second story. And between them, just ahead, was what Pug called, the Great Room. To the right, a river stone fireplace rose two stories. To the left were forest green sofas, overstuffed chairs, cherry end tables, and a foosball and pool table. A giant TV screen filled the wall. But the real attraction was the glittering Pacific directly ahead—the light reflecting off it, blazing through a glass wall, bathing everything in an orange-red sunset.

Well, that was the real attraction for me. Chip's entered through a side door—soaking wet, long, tangled, jet-black hair. A teenage minx (do people still use that word?) in a white, one-piece bathing suit so sheer it was barely needed. "Hey London?" Pug called.

She gave only the vaguest indication of hearing, and even less of caring, as she walked past, leaving wet footprints on the slate.

"How's surf?" he asked.

She answered, her voice flat with boredom. "The usual."

"Cool."

She continued toward the stairs when Chip finally regained enough consciousness to ask, "You surf?" It was a desperate question, asked by a desperate teen. And, though his voice cracked a bit, you had to give the kid credit for courage. She gave no answer and started up the steps. Just as well. Everything about her spelled trouble.

Pug called after her. "This is Dr. Will Thomas. He's going to be on your dad's show tomorrow."

Another step of uninterest, before slowing. She turned and, for the first time, acknowledged our presence. "The mysterious Miracle Man?"

Pug gave me a wink. "Looks like you got a new handle, bro."

Before I could respond, Chip stepped in. "I'm his associate, Chip Brunswick."

She turned her gaze upon him.

He swallowed. "Like his manager. The guy who arranges it all."

She said nothing—simply looked at me then back to him. Finally, she asked, "You surf?"

"Of course. It's been a while but I—" Chip coughed. "I could always brush up with a few pointers."

She turned and continued up the stairs.

He called after her, "I mean if you had the time. Helping me to brush up, I mean."

Another step in silence before, not looking back, she answered, "We'll see."

Chip refrained from leaping into the air, though he did give a fist pump while mouthing, *Yes!* like he'd just won the lotto. Maybe he had. As one male honoring another, I chose to let him bask in the victory—at least until dinner when I'd ask if he'd checked in on Amber.

ço

My respect for Trevor Hunter did not increase when Pug introduced me to my room—oval, king-size bed, original art work, a polished beryl wood desk, marble tub complete with Jacuzzi, and a majestic view of the Pacific (that I could lighten or darken with an electronic remote). And the floor? Still slate. But heated, Pug explained, so bare feet would never touch cold stone. Chip's room was identical. Yes sir, all the basic necessities thanks to the hard-earned donations of folks helping to spread the gospel.

Dinner fared no better. We were escorted to the dining room where we met Cheri—a female version of Pug, but with a British accent. She wore a turquoise top with a white, pleated tennis skirt, modestly covering her long, bronzed legs. Chip and I were directed to opposite sides of a twelve-foot mahogany table complete with china, silverware, and crystal goblets. All that was missing were the candlesticks.

"Where is everybody?" Chip asked as we took our seats.

"Trev sends his apologies," Cheri said. "He should be here any moment. He has, however, asked that you start without him."

"And Jordan?" I said. "Will his wife be joining us?"

Chip quickly added, "And London?"

"I'm afraid not," Cheri said. "Schedules, you know."

Although he was disappointed, it seemed to have little effect upon another one of Chip's major priorities. "So, when do we eat?"

"For this evening, Chef has prepared two choices. Tofu Katsu Curry, one of my favorites, or if you're an animal eater, California's famous barbecued tri-tip with garlic green—" She came to a stop as someone in the hallway caught her attention. "Ah, here he is now."

I heard the clank and scraping of chains a moment before he appeared. Trevor Hunter was no less imposing in person than on TV. A tan, carved body in cargo pants and white designer polo shirt. But it was the shackles that surprised me. Around his wrists were thick, iron cuffs connected by a three-foot chain. Larger cuffs were clasped around each of his ankles and connected by a longer chain.

"Hey, Cheri." He shuffled past, gently brushing the small of her back.

She stiffened. "Trev." You didn't have to be a miracle man to sense something between them.

Trevor turned to us, all grins. "Will!" He approached, dragging his chains. I rose and, as he reached to shake my hand, the restraints dissolved. "How awesome you could find the time to join us."

"The pleasure is all mine," I said (hating how celebrities bring out the panderer in me).

"I'm Chip Brunswick," Chip said, rising to his feet. "Dr. Thomas's associate."

"Ah," Trevor said as he crossed around the table to shake his hand, "Chip Brunswick, agent extraordinaire." Still grinning, he turned to me. "Can't tell you how many times your man was on the phone with my people."

"Yes," I said, "he can be quite . . . ambitious."

He turned back to Chip and chuckled, "Name of the game, right dude?"

"You got that right, Trev."

I tried not to wince.

"And thanks for coming in a day early," Trevor said. "We can hang tomorrow, fill me in as we get ready for the show."

"Right," I said. Unable to hide my anxiety, I repeated, "The show."

Another grin. "No worries, dude. You'll crush it."

Chip turned to me, "He's right, dude, you've got this nailed."

"Listen," Trevor glanced at his watch, "I've got a monster call coming in. From the governor, if you can believe it."

"Of . . . California?" Chip asked.

"Yeah, crazy, huh."

"Governor Proctor? He may run for president."

"That's what I hear."

If Chip was starstruck before, he was downright speechless now. A first if I recall.

"So," Trevor said. "If you don't mind, I'll leave you in Cheri's very capable hands. But let's do breakfast tomorrow. Hang out all morning if you want. Lots I wanna hear."

I nodded. "Alright."

"Fantastic. Okay, gotta bounce." He turned for the door. "You guys are the best."

"No prob, Trev," Chip called after him, "Glory to God, right?"

Without turning, Trevor gave a thumbs up. As he passed Cheri, he nodded, "Cheri."

"Trev."

He disappeared down the hall. And that was that. In two minutes, the great Trevor Hunter had made his grand entrance and exit. All that remained was the sound of his rattling and scraping chains fading into the distance.

CHAPTER

FOURTEEN

"WILL, THAT'S JUST not how the Lord works."

I sat on the edge of the bed talking to Patricia over my phone. Outside, the moon was nearly full, lighting up the pounding surf. I'd called Patricia, glad she picked up—but not exactly thrilled about the conversation.

"Trust me," I said. "It's not how I work either."

"And yet, there you are, all over the internet, trying to mimic Joseph Namaliu—again.

"Mimic?

"Raising a baby from the dead.

"Patricia, I wasn't trying to—"

"He's a devout man of God, Will. He has given his entire life to studying and humbly serving our Lord."

No argument there. The little miracle worker from Papua New Guinea who once shared a Sunday meal with us was the real deal. Granted, he'd not been able to heal Billie-Jean, but there was an honest humility about him, not to mention a gentle power.

"You don't see him showing off on the internet."

"No," I ran a hand through my hair. "No, of course not."

"And yet, there you are. Everywhere."

I closed my eyes.

"You're all my students talk about, Will. The ones who have taken courses from you are practically celebrities."

"It's nothing I planned."

"And you've only known the Lord for what, a year?"

There was a knock on the door. I rose to answer. "Actually, less than—"

"I'm simply telling you it's a trap."

"A trap?"

"The devil is very clever and I fear he has found a way to seduce you."

"Seduce?" I opened the door to see Chip. He brushed past me.

She continued, "You've lost your job, your reputation, everything you worked so hard for. Seriously, I can appreciate your discomfort. So now he's tempting you with a little fame. It's only natural for you to want to repair your reputation."

Chip moved to the window. Even with his back to me I could see he was agitated.

"Patricia, you saw what happened in front of the church. What the student said."

"Which I've yet to understand."

"And now that baby. I mean, if he really was dead . . ." I let the phrase hang, unsure how to finish it.

"*For Satan himself masquerades as an angel of light.*"

"You've said that before, but—"

"It's in the Bible. You're being deceived, Will. The devil is puffing you up with pride by deceiving you with counterfeits."

Chip turned, motioning for me to wrap up.

I frowned at him and continued. "What about Trevor Hunter? He seems to think—"

"I'm not so convinced about Trevor Hunter either. After listening to his sermons, I mean really listening—all he talks about is God's love."

"Is that a problem?"

"What about sin? Repentance? The call for holiness?"

I had no answer, not uncommon around her.

She continued. "Darlene has always had her doubts about him, and the more I study him, the more I agree."

"Will?" Chip whispered.

I motioned for another minute. He turned back to the window.

"So what do you want me to do?" I asked.

"Come home. Renounce all this nonsense and come home."

"You don't think I should do tomorrow's show?"

"It's not my place to tell you what to do. Pray about it. Let your conscience be your guide. And while you're at it, consider the impact your actions are having upon others, especially all those young people."

"I—"

"It's getting late. I have an early class tomorrow."

"Right, but—"

"I need to call it a night."

"Alright."

"Pray, Will. Pray very hard."

"Okay, but—"

"Good night."

"Patricia?" There was no answer. "Patricia, are you there?" I shook my head, paused then slowly disconnected.

Chip turned to me, his face filled with anxiety. "Can I stay here and sleep with you?"

"Can you— Why, what's wrong?"

"Pug, he came to my room." Chip started to pace.

"And?"

"He dropped off London's key."

"London? Trevor's daughter?"

"Says, 'Hey, little dude. Got a gift for you.' And I go, 'Gift?' And he goes, 'She's waiting.' And I like, for a second, I don't get it and he says, 'It's cool. She's cool. But I'd strike while the iron is hot, if you know what I mean.'"

"Pug said that?"

Chip nodded.

"And what did you do?"

"I passed. I said, 'Thanks but, you know, I got a girl.' And he says, 'It's cool whatever you decide, no problem. I'll just leave the key here in case you change your mind.'"

"So, why are you—"

"Ten minutes later she's knocking on my door. And . . . and . . ." He took a breath.

"And you said?"

"No. Of course I said no. But she's like real clear what she wants, and I say, 'What about your dad?' and she goes, 'He's the last person who'll mind,' and I, I still say no. I mean I know what the Bible says. But she's—" He stopped and took another breath. "You see how hot she is."

"So . . . you want to stay here with me?"

"It's a big bed. If you want, I can sleep right there on the floor."

I could only stare. Despite my best efforts, my estimation of Chip Brunswick's character continued to grow.

CHAPTER
FIFTEEN

NO MATTER HOW I tried, sleep would not come. And it wasn't just Chip's cold feet. Much of it had to do with Patricia's phone call—not just about me (which was enough), but about Trevor. In the name of love was he really excluding key elements of the gospel? What about his encouragement for people to go into debt so he could live in luxury? And his daughter? I know you can't always judge a parent by their children (Adam and Eve being God's kids a prime example). But what did she mean about Trevor being the last person to care if she slept around?

And yet, by the way Trevor Hunter Ministries continued to flourish—he must be doing something right.

All this kept churning in my head until I finally had to get up and take a pre-dawn walk along the beach. Of course, I hoped Yeshua would show to make sense of it, but after forty or so minutes I gave up and retraced my steps to the castle. I was surprised to see two young joggers, girls in their early twenties who could have easily passed for my students back home. They'd stopped at the water's edge looking down. I heard the anger in their voices and, as I approached, I saw it in their faces. A seagull lay gasping at their feet. Its legs were tangled in clear, plastic webbing, the type used to hold six-packs together.

"Unbelievable," the shorter of the two scorned.

"People," the taller agreed. "So thoughtless."

"It's so cruel. So, so . . ."

"Barbaric."

"Should we call animal control?"

As I passed, they looked up, the taller one calling to me. "Can you believe it?"

I shook my head in agreement.

"People, they have no respect for life."

Suddenly, a familiar voice said, "Ask them if they're pro-choice."

I looked to see Yeshua walking beside me. "What?" I whispered.

"Ask them."

I frowned. He nodded. Having learned it's usually better to do things his way, I slowed to a stop and called back to them. "May I ask you a question?"

They looked up and waited.

"Are you . . ." I hesitated.

"Go ahead," Yeshua said.

"Are you pro-choice?"

They stared.

"Ask again."

Seriously? I thought.

"Again."

I cleared my throat. "Are you . . . just curious, are you pro-choice?"

They traded looks. "Of course," the taller one scoffed. "What's that got to do with anything?"

I waited for a prompt, some answer from Yeshua; after all, it was his idea. But he said nothing, leaving the three of us standing in silence, save for the pounding surf.

Figuring it best to ignore the crazy old-timer, they turned back to the bird and I resumed my walk, muttering, "That went nicely."

"It will," Yeshua said. "Your question will haunt one of them and, in time, it will save one of her children."

Although I had a vague idea what he meant, it wasn't high on my list of concerns. I changed subjects. "Why do you leave me on my own so much?" I asked.

"I never leave you."

"Right, but these special guest appearances, they don't always come when I need them."

"When you *think* you need them. What you're learning, Will, is to rely on the same power I had; the same power available to anyone."

"And that power is . . . ?"

He looked out to the ocean and I followed his gaze. There was the Spirit, in bright, Hawaiian board shorts, surfing a wave that grew larger and larger as he motioned to it. Needless to say, he had no board.

"Are you kidding?" I said.

"When I was in your world, he's all I had."

"Right, but you're the Son of God."

"Who had the same limitations as you . . . and the same power."

I gave a start when the Spirit appeared, walking at my other side. "He's always here to empower you, Will. And to refresh. Consider him a portable well, always available to drink from."

"And by drink you mean . . . ?"

"To abide with us. Commune. To enjoy our peace and our power."

As is often the case, he fell into silence, letting me digest the depth of his meaning. We eventually reached the beach entrance to the castle. That's when I noticed the smell, like burnt matches.

"What is that?" I asked.

Yeshua sniffed the air. "Sulfur."

"It's the same thing I smelled back at the hospital when—AUGH!" I shouted and stopped. Just ahead, rising from the floor of the castle's open doorway, stretched a half dozen spindly arms. "They're back!"

"Oh, those," Yeshua said. "Not to worry. They're always around."

More arms sprouted—not only from the floor but from both sides of the opening, as well as its top—glistening in the moonlight, their razor-sharp claws slashing the air.

"I can't go through there!"

"Sure you can."

"No, I—"

"He who is in you is greater than he who is in the—"

"Impossible!" I cried. The arms continued to grow and multiply, creating a blockade of writhing flesh and snapping talons. "Look!" I pointed. "Look!"

"No, Will," Yeshua calmly replied. "You look."

I was blinded by sunlight. As my eyes adjusted, I saw we stood in a rocky alcove shaded by a couple trees. Before us was a tent with ten, maybe fifteen men dressed like biblical warriors—swords, battered helmets, metal coats. They were scoffing and snickering at some scrawny teen who staggered around in similar garb several times too large for him.

"Where are we?" I whispered.

"Remember the five steps?"

"Things have been a little bit crazy."

"Step One—accepting my promise? Step Two, ridicule by those closest to you?"

It was all coming back. "Step Three," I said, "making it happen on my own."

"Doing it your way instead of mine."

"No matter how illogical."

Ignoring the last comment, he motioned back to the scene. The kid was ripping off his helmet, complaining, "It doesn't fit, I can't fight with these."

The men laughed, taunting him, "So what are you going to do, little brother?"

The boy looked past the trees down to a small ravine. "I'm going to that stream and getting me some stones. I'm going to put an end to that big-mouth giant."

I turned to Yeshua. "Stones . . . giant? Is that David?"

He answered, "Step four. Obedience. Doing it my way."

Suddenly, we were perched on an outcropping of rock. Above us stood hundreds of soldiers yelling and jeering. Not far below, David was facing the giant and shouting, "*It's not by sword or spear that the Lord saves; for the battle is the Lord's!*" Gathering himself, he charged at the big man.

I watched, preparing to see firsthand the drama we'd all heard since we were kids, but I was back on the beach, facing the wall of waving arms and claws—and now faces. Individual faces began to appear—part reptilian, part frog.

"No!" I shook my head. "I'm not some Bible hero. I don't have that kind of faith!"

"It's not your faith, Will." He motioned to the Spirit beside me. "It's ours. I'm its author. I'm its perfector."

The faces continued to emerge, bulging eyes, mouths with needle-sharp fangs, their growls growing to cries then shrieking screams.

Yeshua shouted, "Whose battle is this?"

My heart pounded. I could barely breathe.

"Whose battle, Will?"

"Yours," I gasped.

"Whose power?"

"Yours."

"My battle! My power!"

I took a breath. My whole body trembled. I turned to Yeshua and the Spirit. Both quietly nodded. My shaking continued. But somehow, some way, by keeping my eyes on them, I was finally able to return their nods. And, instantly, there came the sound of ringing steel. Soldiers appeared around me. Instead of guns they drew swords. And, directly in front, taking the lead, was Gideon's warrior. My warrior. He looked back at me, sword in hand, waiting.

I took another breath and stepped toward the doorway of screaming creatures. As I entered, the carnage began. Brutal. Arms hacked off. Dismembered limbs gushing putrid blood as they fell away. Decapitated heads shrieking as they fell, hissing and turning to vapor before hitting the ground. I hesitated once, maybe twice. Both times the soldiers paused with me. When I continued, they continued.

Was I in danger? Every second. Was I ever touched? Half a dozen times a claw brushed my face, even a fang—just before swords appeared severing and destroying them. Not a drop of blood was shed—at least mine.

How long did it take for me to walk through the entrance? How long do nightmares last? But as the final scream faded, as the last arm fell to the ground and evaporated, the soldiers dissolved, disappeared. Only the smell of sulfur remained and only for a moment.

"Uncle Will."

I was shocked to see Chip standing on the other side of the doorway. Swallowing, struggling for composure, I finally said, "You're up early."

"You too."

"I couldn't sleep."

"Me neither," he said. "I had this crazy dream."

I was too shaken to show interest as we started down the hallway. But it didn't stop Chip from sharing. "You and me, we were in this battle, fighting at the mouth of this gonzo monster thing." I'd had enough of battles and remained silent as we entered the Great Hall starting for the stairs. "And there were like these bad boy soldiers with swords all around us. And this one, the baddest of all, he had like this scar running from his ear all the way down to his chin. Gnarly dude."

I slowed, but he wasn't quite finished.

"And what's with that smell? Back at the entrance, did you smell it? Like rotten eggs or burnt matches or something. Didn't you smell it?"

CHAPTER
SIXTEEN

I WAS SURPRISED Chip smelled the sulfur and asked if there was anything else he remembered about it or his dream. He didn't, but said it was so detailed it almost seemed real. And it was in color. "Did you know most men don't dream in color?" he said. I didn't and didn't much care—though I did add Chip's experience to my "Now What Are You Up To?" list.

With time to kill before breakfast, he suggested we do some exploring. I wanted to change and take a shower first and suggested he go back to his room and do the same.

"Cool," he said. "I'll wait."

We started down in the basement where we found a single-lane bowling alley, a racquetball court, and an adjoining sauna with shower. At the other end was an impressive library, glass-enclosed wine cellar, and a private movie theater with a dozen leather recliners. The main floor was pretty much devoted to the Great Hall, with two hallways—one leading to the dining room, the other to the beach entrance. But it was the second story with its guest suites and living quarters that held the greatest surprise.

For the record, Chip insisted we weren't exactly snooping, just checking things out. Call it what you will, but we had no business in the hallway to the living quarters when we stumbled upon a love-starved couple passionately kissing each other in what must have been morning goodbyes. She, a tall, ruby-haired beauty standing, nearly open-robed, in a suite's doorway. He, a clothed and bearded model right out of GQ. We couldn't make out the faces which were pretty much glued together and too preoccupied to notice our appearance—and hasty disappearance.

It wasn't until we were out of earshot in the opposite wing and safely in my room that Chip suggested, "Probably guests. Newlyweds saying goodbye before he goes to work."

I nodded.

"Young love," he mused, shaking his head.

Later, over breakfast, a more likely explanation surfaced. Once again Trevor was unable to join us. Cheri explained it was because of some fantastic news he wanted to personally share with us next door at the studio, "Say, 9:00 a.m.?" she asked.

"That's fine," I said.

"And that's when he'll provide a rundown for tonight's show?" Chip asked. "It's important Dr. Thomas and I have a detailed itinerary should any extraneous circumstances arise during the course of the evening's taping."

Suppressing a smile, Cheri explained, "Actually, we tape the show in the early afternoon should there be a need for retakes. Then, of course, there is the East Coast's three-hour time difference."

"Of course," Chip said. "That goes without saying."

"But I shall have a schedule in your hands by noon."

"Thank you."

"In the meantime, please enjoy your—" she looked over to my plate, "eggs benedict." Then to Chip's, "And your—"

"Steak and eggs," Chip said. "And tell Chef he has once again outdone himself."

"Certainly." Preparing to exit she repeated, "9:00 a.m., then. Enjoy your morning, gentlemen." She turned and nearly bumped into— "Jordan. Good morning."

A tall, slender woman in her late thirties stepped into the room, her voice clogged with morning thickness. "Good morning."

Cheri motioned to us. "Have you met our guests yet?"

She turned to us and broke into a blinding smile. "Ah, the Miracle Man from Washington State." Stunned at what I saw, I still managed to rise. "Please sit, sit," she said. Turning to Chip, she added, "And you are his—"

For the second time in as many days Chip was speechless. But, unlike London, it was not because of the woman's beauty. It was because of the ruby-red hair, the very same hair we'd seen an hour earlier in the hallway.

She smiled. "Well whoever you are," she said, pulling up a chair and sitting, "my daughter says you're quite the looker." With a flirtatious smile she added, "And I see she wasn't wrong."

"Chip," he finally croaked.

"Well, Chip, I trust you two had an enjoyable evening."

"Yes," he said. "I mean no, I mean . . ." She waited, throwing me a knowing wink as he continued. "We're just friends, I mean that would be great—being friends I mean, but—we didn't . . ."

She laughed. "Trust me. I know my daughter."

"But we—"

She reached out to pat his hand. "Count yourself lucky, she can be very selective." Before he could respond, she turned back to Cheri who remained standing near the exit. "Please, Cheri, I'll have the usual."

"Certainly, Jordan." Cheri turned and headed into the kitchen.

Finally, mustering the presence to string two words together, and never guilty of having manners, Chip asked, "You approve of her behavior?"

Jordan turned back to him.

He swallowed then continued, "You know."

She smiled sweetly. "It's London's body. She's nineteen. She can do with it whatever she wants."

"Right, but . . ."

She waited.

"I mean the Bible; it says having sex with someone if you're not married to them—"

"Is wrong?" she said.

"Yes."

"Scripture also says Jesus loves and forgives no matter what we do. And in today's world, not to mention the raging hormones of youth . . ." She let the phrase hang, leaving Chip unsure how to answer. Turning back to me, she asked, "So did Trev tell you the terrific news?"

"Terrific news?" I said.

But Chip, in his irritating persistence, wouldn't let go. "I'm sorry." Jordan turned to him and he continued, "Jesus also says our righteousness has to be greater than the scribes and Pharisees. It's right there in the Bible somewhere."

I gave Chip a scowl. This was obviously not the time. Then again, any time Chip had something to say seemed the right time for him.

Jordan was unfazed. "And which are you?"

"Which am I?"

"Are you a scribe or Pharisee?"

"That's not what I mean."

"Doesn't Jesus clearly say, *Let him without sin cast the first stone? Judge not, lest ye be judged*?" She turned to me. "Am I right, Doctor?"

I wasn't sure how to respond. Diplomacy called for a certain tact. But, looking to Chip, I had the strange feeling my tact might be an excuse for cowardness.

Turning back to him, she said, "You see, Chad, it's that type of attitude that's causing people, especially young people like yourself, to flee the church. In droves. Jesus Christ said he came into the world, not to judge, but to forgive." She looked back to me, waiting for agreement. I was grateful for a second chance to agree with Chip. To my embarrassment, I settled for a knowing smile. A knowing smile! What was wrong with me!?

She continued, "It's all about love. That's what Jesus taught. And forgiveness. I mean look at Trev. The poor guy is so busy he barely knows I exist. Much less London. But I don't hold that against him. Look at all he's doing for God. I totally forgive him."

To Chip's credit he tried again. "But that's not—the Bible doesn't just say—"

"And Trev totally forgives me."

Chip turned to me for help.

"It's . . . complicated," I mumbled. Strike three!

"Exactly," she agreed. "And we're a complicated people. So God totally gets—" she was interrupted by Cheri entering with a small tray of six poached shrimp. "Oh, wonderful," she said as Cheri set it before her. Picking up a small fork with what must have been a prayer, "Thank you, Jesus," she dug in.

Chip and I said nothing.

She closed her eyes and sighed, "Heaven. You two really have to try these." She continued chewing. "Only thirteen calories apiece, a girl's dream." As she spoke, Cheri set a thick glass of what looked like tomato juice before her. "Thanks, Cheri," she said. "It's going to be a long day. Better make that two."

Cheri nodded and disappeared back into the kitchen. I stared hard at my breakfast.

So," she bit into another shrimp, "Let's not focus on the negative, okay? We're all friends here. Brothers and sisters in Christ. Right? Am I right?"

Chip gave a vague, half-confused, half-defeated nod.

"So let's have ourselves a nice little breakfast and celebrate."

I finally spoke. "Celebrate?"

"Oh, you didn't hear? The governor's coming in to do Trev's show tonight!"

"Governor Proctor?" I asked.

"Isn't that fantastic?" she exclaimed. "You have any idea what this will do for our ratings? Somebody as powerful as Governor Proctor?"

Taking a sip, she added, "Voted most eligible bachelor in America?" She growled a comedic, "Meow." At least I thought it comedic. Regardless, Chip and I traded glances as she grinned and raised her glass in a toast. "Cheers!"

CHAPTER
SEVENTEEN

CHIP AND I returned to my room in silence. But instead of enjoying the peace and quiet, I went against my better judgment and asked, "Are you okay?"

He looked up, startled from his thoughts. "Yeah . . . I'm fine."

But he wasn't fine. Neither was I.

Things got no better when we walked next door to meet Trevor at the studio. The place was everything the castle wasn't. Except for the affluence. Instead of medieval stone, the outside was sleek glass and steel. It seemed to rise from the sand like a buried spaceship. We were a few minutes early so Dylan, a young assistant, barely older than Chip, was summoned to give us a tour. He wore the standard uniform of sandals, cargo pants, and polo shirt. His missing left arm and painfully pronounced limp made it clear Trevor wasn't focused on just hiring "the beautiful people." A definite plus. But looking about the plush audience seating, the state-of-the-art equipment, including TV cameras on remote-controlled pedestals, only increased the paradox of Trever Hunter Ministries.

"And this is where the magic happens," Dylan said as we descended the steps to an elaborate set of fake steel girders, AC vents, and a steel and glass desk. To the right were two elevated rows for the band. I was struck by how everything looked smaller in person than on TV.

"What are those?" I motioned to our left where a dozen desks sat.

"The phone banks for our donation drives." With a chuckle Dylan added, "Sometimes we just sit there talking to friends, you know, pretending to take calls—just for show."

"Right?" Chip mumbled, looking around, "What isn't."

"Pardon me?"

He shook his head. Noting the sullenness, Dylan walked behind Trevor's desk and pulled out the chair. "Wanna try out the throne?"

"I'm good," Chip said.

"Go ahead, Trev won't mind."

Before he could answer, a woman's voice called from one side of the set. "Dylan?" We turned and saw a young woman approach. Even with head down, examining her iPad, I recognized her as one of the girls I'd met on the beach. "The governor's advance team will be here in thirty. I'm sending you a list of requested green room supplies."

"Roger that," Dylan said.

"And a revised script." She continued studying her iPad as she crossed the stage.

"Revised?"

"He's replacing the healer dude. Sophie will contact his people."

"Um . . ." Before Dylan could explain, she was gone. He turned to me, unsure what to say.

I saved him the effort. "'Healer dude.' I'm guessing that's me?"

He gave a helpless shrug. "Sorry."

"And so am I!" We turned to the opposite door where Trevor, one sleeve rolled up, was emerging. At his side walked a petite blonde, slightly flushed, discreetly touching her hair. He continued, "Not only sorry, but embarrassed. Believe me, it was the last thing I anticipated or wanted."

I had my doubts but nodded.

"We'll make it up to you," he said as they approached. "I swear."

"These things happen," I said.

He shook his head, adding, "You have my word." He saw Chip and grinned. "Hey, sport."

Eyeing the girl and obviously thinking the worst, Chip flatly said, "Hi."

Rolling down his sleeve, Trevor made introductions. "This is Elizabeth Muncy, my personal assistant and part-time drug dealer." She laughed. He continued, "And, Liz, this is Dr. Will Thomas, the Miracle Man from Seattle."

She reached out and shook my hand. "I've heard lots about you."

"Thanks." It was a stupid thing to say but the best I could come up with.

"And his number one man, Chip."

Chip nodded and looked down.

Referring to his sleeve as he adjusted it, Trevor explained, "Just a little Vitamin B to keep things going—since we've run out of the IV stands for coffee."

Elizabeth grinned. "He's such a baby, he needs me to do the injections."

"You're good at it."

"They say sleep helps too," she replied.

"Someday, kiddo," he said. "Someday. So, are we done here?"

She nodded. "I'll make those calls you requested." Turning to us she said, "It was nice meeting you both." I nodded, saying the same, and she headed for the door calling to Trevor, "Text me if you need anything."

"Always," Trevor called back, then to us added, "Great kid. A real go-getter."

I smiled, giving him the benefit of the doubt. Chip's verdict had already been reached.

Trevor turned to Dylan. "Hey, Dill, mind if I steal these two away for a minute?"

"No prob, Trev."

"Fantastic. Before things get too crazy, there's something I want to show them." Throwing an arm around my shoulder, he turned us toward the office. "You comin', Chip?"

"I'm good," Chip said, pretending to look about the room.

"Got it," Trevor said. "Want to enjoy the God vibe, right?" Before Chip could answer, he added, "Don't blame you, lots of cool stuff happens here."

"But you . . ." He pulled me in tighter, as we headed across the set. "Be prepared to have your mind blown."

CHAPTER
EIGHTEEN

THE SHACKLES WERE back on Trevor's wrists and ankles as he dragged the chains around his office enthusiastically explaining the myriad of blueprints, sketches, and drawings pinned to nearly every wall. I sat on a leather sofa watching the presentation, while across the room Yeshua leaned against a desk overflowing with paperwork. In the center, atop a glass table, sat a two-foot model of Las Vegas's famous Cube—an indoor arena cleverly designed to rest on one point with all four walls stretching out then up.

"Wave Field Synthesis, 120,000 speakers, 300 by 300-foot screens on each of the four walls, 16K resolution—the ultimate immersive experience. Nobody, I mean nobody, has had a revival like this."

"Revival?" I asked.

"Revival. Pep rally. You name it. Top musicians, dancers, everything off the charts. And the best part, are you ready for this?" He moved to the model, his chains dragging behind. "When I'm all done preaching, when I get everybody pumped for Jesus, the dude himself, will make his grand appearance!"

I threw a startled look to Yeshua. He simply shrugged.

Trevor, seeing my expression, added, "You know, the Second Coming."

"The Second—"

"Projected on all four walls, the ceiling, the floor." He opened the walls of the Cube to reveal the screens and seating. "Thousands of singing angels descending with him, saints riding white steeds, 4-D immersion with hurricane wind, Haptic technology, the seats shaking like an earthquake! Think Superbowl halftime on steroids!"

"You're using live actors?"

"A few to keep the union off our back. The rest is all AI *except . . .*" He produced a small doll complete with robe and beard. "Descending through the roof, all ninety-three feet, six inches of him," he lowered the doll through the opening, "a live, holographic projection of Jesus Christ!"

I looked over to Yeshua. He could only shake his head. Then he motioned to the back of my sofa. I turned and saw the Spirit sitting on the back and to my right, still in his surfer attire. In his hands he held a bolt cutter—the type used for cutting chains.

"You with me, Will?"

I turned back to him. "You said, live."

"We're negotiating with, well I can't tell you who just yet, but he's big. Academy Award–winning big."

I stole another glance to Yeshua who struck a pose like a movie star, thoughtfully stroking his beard. Obviously, heaven humor.

"So what do you think?"

I had no idea where to start.

"Speechless, right?"

I stared at the model. "Who is paying for all this?"

"The people, dude. All those kids who love Jesus and want to show him to the world. And, oh, this is cool. I just thought of it, so call it a God thing."

Yeshua dropped his head it into his hand.

"If you want in, listen— If you want, we can include your ministry in the advertising because we're going to be all over the city."

"My . . . ministry?"

"Sure. The more the merrier. And after stiffing you on this gig, which again, I couldn't be sorrier, we can work out something really reasonable."

I frowned. "We don't, I mean, we really can't—"

"No, I get it, money's tight. None of this pays for itself, right? It's like you and me, we're on this giant hamster wheel running as fast as we can." He motioned to the room and the studio beyond. "But that's what this is all about, right? If you want people to know God's a winner, you got to show them what winning looks like."

I felt the Spirit nudge me and I turned to see him offering the bolt cutter.

"But baby, the expenses, right? I mean, just between us, 'Mano of God a Mano of God,' what's your monthly nut?"

"My . . . ?"

"Operational expense."

"We're pretty small."

"Right, how small?"

"Well, there's me and . . ."

"And the kid, and . . ." He waited for more. I had nothing.

"You're joking," he said.

"No. That's about it."

He whistled, then dragged his chains over to sit beside me. "With all the coverage you're getting, dude? I had no idea. Amazing. And starting out at your age."

Tell me about it, I thought.

Trevor shook his head.

I watched as Yeshua slipped off the desk and strolled over to us.

"Amazing," Trevor repeated. Then, after a moment, he softly added, "But you know, I gotta tell you, part of me envies you." As he spoke, Yeshua kneeled to our feet. "When me and Jordan were starting off, things were tough—you know, living in a trailer, beater car, macaroni and cheese days. But they were good too. No bottom-line worries. When we talked to people on the street we could talk gospel, you know what I mean? Just pure gospel."

I watched as Yeshua reached down to take the chain wrapped around Trevor's ankles. It clinked and rattled as he raised it toward me. He motioned to the bolt cutter in the Spirit's hand, indicating I should take it. Suddenly, finally, I understood. I didn't like it, but I understood. He wanted me to say something. He expected me to tell Trevor the very thing he'd been teaching me—the difference between doing God's work God's way or trying to do it ours.

There was nothing wrong with Trevor's goals; they were noble. But like Abraham, like me, like so many others, his methods were wrong. And the results? I saw it now. A ministry more dedicated to keeping itself afloat than serving others. A fractured family riddled with immorality. And a gospel that, according to Patricia, may not even be the gospel.

But how could I, of all people, tell him? Me, a disgraced, unemployed teacher. Me, a newbie with no Bible training. And let's not forget my questionable and far-too-public record. As the truth took shape, becoming more obvious, I noticed the faint odor of burnt matches. The sulfur. I looked back down to Yeshua. He was still holding the chain up to me. But this time, my response was firm. There would be no budging. There were hundreds, thousands of men and women far more qualified to correct him. Trevor Hunter was the leader of an exploding ministry, an inspiration for an entire generation. And he was about to be visited by a governor, a possible candidate for president of the United States of America. No way was I the one to lecture him.

"Repent and be saved." I turned to Trevor who continued, lost in his own thoughts. "That's what it was all about. Turn to Jesus and stop sinning. But now," he shook his head. "You know the last time I talked about sin? I can't even tell you. Now everything has to be positive and upbeat."

I felt a firmer nudge against my shoulder, the Spirit with the bolt cutter—as the smell of sulfur grew—as Trevor continued, even more quietly. "*The wages of sin is death but the gift of God is eternal life in Christ Jesus our Lord.*" Once again, he shook his head. "Well, half the gospel is better than none, right? I mean God is love, right? That's what sells. That's what feeds the machine and keeps it running."

I said nothing, refusing to let my eyes meet Yeshua's and ignoring the Spirit's request to take the bolt cutter. Finally, Trevor rose to his feet. He stepped around the kneeling Yeshua, dragging his chains over to the model. "And with this puppy they're going to get the message loud and clear—all ninety-three feet of him. God is love! Right? God . . . is . . . love!" With a trace of irony he added, "If we can just convince his agent to charge us a reasonable fee."

I sensed commotion behind me and turned to see the Spirit beginning to fade. I looked down to Yeshua. He was doing the same.

"Hello?" I turned to see Trevor, his back to me, his finger pressed against the Bluetooth in his ear. "What? No way! No! I'll be right there. No, no, no! Tell him I'm on my way."

He disconnected from the call and turned back to me. "Sorry, man. More union stuff." Reaching for the model, he closed up the four walls. "No rest for the righteous, right?"

I took my cue and rose stiffly to my feet.

"Anyway," he said, "please accept my apologies for tonight. We'll get you back on the show as soon as sched-ules permit." He crossed to me and, draping an arm over my shoulder, turned us to the door. "See if we can increase that donor base of yours. And, like I said, if you want a piece of the action, let me know. Could be just the kick-start you need."

I nodded and took a final look to the sofa and floor. All trace of Yeshua and the Spirit were gone. Only a whiff of sulfur remained.

CHAPTER
NINETEEN

THEY HUSTLED US off the grounds as quickly as possible. Not that I blamed them. All hands had to be on deck for Robert Proctor, California governor, and possible presidential candidate. To be honest, as Pug herded us toward the waiting van (the Alfa Romeo and Lamborghini needed to be available should the need arise), I was relieved. The sooner we left the compound, the sooner I could put both Trevor's operation and my own guilt out of mind. (Well, one out of two wasn't bad.) Truth is, I seldom said no to Yeshua. His way was usually best—eventually. And I always felt better agreeing—eventually. But not this time. This time, because of basic decency and politeness (spelled, c-o-w-a-r-d), I remained the silent, well-behaved guest, refusing to become one of those judgmental Pharisees.

And my insides were already paying the price.

I thanked Cheri for her hospitality, left a note for Trevor saying I'd be praying, even offered to help the staff clean our rooms and load our stuff into the van. But no matter what I did, the heaviness would not leave my chest. Chip's mood was no better. Meanwhile, as if mocking, the noonday weather was bright, cheery, and sunny.

We'd just pulled from the palm-lined drive onto Pacific Coast Highway when Chip, riding shotgun, said, "What's going on?"

"What's that?" Pug asked."

"Why's everything getting dark?"

"Dark?"

"Where'd the sun go?"

Pug looked up through the windshield. "Right where it's always been."

I left my self-loathing just long enough to see what Chip was talking about. He had a point. Everything was growing dark. Well, not everything. Just the road ahead of us—like a thick, black fog.

"It's coming up fast," Chip said. "Don't you see it?"

Pug chuckled as we entered its dark, wispy edge. "Might wanna cut back your medication, little dude, 'cause I don't see— Hey! There they are, now!"

We were deep inside the blackness when we passed a large SUV. And then it was gone, the dark cloud thinning and evaporating back into bright sunlight.

"That's the governor?" Chip asked.

"Yeah." Pug glanced at his watch. "They're early." He pressed the accelerator.

"What's the hurry?" I called from the back.

"Need to drop you off and head back to help Cheri."

"You seem to have plenty of staff," I said.

"Hospitality's more a me and Cheri thing. We're pretty tight."

I wasn't sure what that meant but with morning suspicions running high, I let it go. Unfortunately, "letting go" was not one of Chip's specialties.

"Cheri?" he said.

"What's that?" Pug asked.

"You and Cheri. Are you guys, like, you know . . ."

"I wish. Nah, she's got a bigger fish on the line."

"You mean Trevor?" Chip said.

Pug threw him a glance and gave another chuckle. "Don't ask, don't tell."

"Meaning?"

"Our little code of ethics."

"Which is . . ."

"Don't ask, don't tell." He flashed Chip a grin.

Choosing to say nothing, Chip slumped back into his seat and looked out the window. Of course I wanted to ask Chip about the black cloud he and I just saw, and Pug hadn't, but figured I could wait until our flight to ask about it—along with his dream and the sulfur he claimed to smell. So we rode in relative silence, save for non-stop, Bob Marley—courtesy of Pug's Spotify.

Twenty minutes later we stopped at a light on Century Boulevard, the airport just ahead. From the curb a homeless man approached and tapped on Chip's window. "Change for a vet?" he called.

Chip reached for the window, but Pug hit the lock button.

Chip turned to him. "What are you doing?"

"Don't like to enable 'em," he said.

"Enable?"

The man tapped again.

Chip argued, "A little change isn't going to hurt."

"He needs to work like everyone else." Off Chip's stare, Pug shrugged, "It's illegal for him to be here anyway."

The light turned green and we pulled away.

Our final stop was in front of the terminal. We started unloading while Pug motioned for a couple curbside porters to give us a hand. (I did mention Amber helped us pack, yes?) Meanwhile, Pug produced a gift and handed it to Chip. "A little something we give to our VIPs," he said.

"What is it?"

"Open it, little dude. We got time."

Chip pulled aside the brown paper wrapping and opened the lid to a box. He stared, blinking.

Pug explained, "It's a Trevor Hunter Study Bible."

"Uh, thanks," Chip said, "but I already got one for my girl."

"Cool, but this one is autographed just to you. By name. Check it out."

Chip pulled the Bible from the box, its gilded edges and calf-skin leather identical to Amber's. He opened the cover and read the first page: "To Chip. Blessings, bro. Trev."

Chip looked up. "Thanks . . . bro." He managed to hide the sarcasm, mostly.

Pug grinned. "No prob."

After giving us both one of those athlete, half-hug things, Pug crossed back to the van and climbed in. "Gotta fly," he called. "Love you guys." I smiled, nodded, and watched as he pulled back into traffic, drawing an angry honk from a driver he cut off.

It wasn't until we entered the terminal and stood in security that I noticed Pug's gift was missing. "Where's the Bible?" I asked.

He shrugged.

"Chip?"

"I left it on one of the garbage cans."

"You what?"

"Not in it. On top." Pretending to busy himself with his knapsack, he added. "No sweat. Someone will find it. Someone who believes all that crap."

PART THREE

CHAPTER
TWENTY

"I AM VERY proud of you, Will," Patricia said. "You did the correct thing."

They say men don't need to hear, "I love you" as much as we need to hear, "I'm proud of you." I don't know who "they" are, but they got that one right.

Patricia picked us up from Sea-Tac. For the most part we exchanged pleasantries, avoiding the Trevor Hunter elephant in the room, while Chip remained silent and sulking in the back. It wasn't until we left the ferry terminal and crossed the island for home that she hit me with that bit of praise. And, for the first time in hours, I didn't completely hate myself. But all good things come to an end.

"He had no choice," Chip called from the back. "They canceled him."

Wonderful, I thought. *Now he decides to talk.*

"Proctor did the entire show."

"Will's spot, as well?" Patricia asked.

"Can't blame them," Chip said. "Proctor's Q score is off the charts."

"His what?"

"Marketability. The higher your Q score, the greater your audience. Because increasing numbers is what it's all about." Looking out the window he added, "Christianity at its finest."

Patricia glanced at him through the rearview mirror. "You seemed to have no difficulty with increasing numbers when it pertained to Will."

"Yeah . . . let's just say I saw the light."

Earlier, on the plane, I tried asking Chip about the cloud surrounding the SUV and the smell of sulfur, but all I got was sullen moodiness. Having a hero deposed can do that to a person.

Of course that didn't silence Patricia Swenson, Defender of the Faith. "Do you think the disciples believed that," she asked him, "when they gave up their lives?" I motioned her to go easy but, like Chip, the missionary kid from Papua New Guinea never quite mastered the art of tact. "Or the millions of followers persecuted to this day?"

"Pawns," Chip said.

"Excuse me?"

"Brainless pawns."

"Perhaps when your disposition isn't so foul we'll continue this conversation."

"Don't bet on it."

Patricia looked to me. I shook my head and this time she remained silent, letting the quiet thrum of tires fill the car. Outside, the light turned golden. Late afternoon sun flickered through the branches of thinning leaves. Autumn was on its way. When she could no longer endure the silence, she turned back to me. "Actually, I believe your appearing on the show was an act of providence. It would only add fuel to your growing notoriety."

"You're talking about the UCLA baby post."

"Among the others. People who know nothing about you are making one exaggerated claim after another." I closed my eyes, grateful that home and some sense of sanity lay just around the bend. "It's better a respected Christian leader like Governor Proctor appear on that show than someone like . . . well someone with your inexperience."

"Wait," I said. "Proctor is a Christian?"

"Indeed he is."

I turned to Chip. "You knew this?"

He shrugged.

"Should the man run for president, he'd certainly have my vote."

"Because he's some hottie?" Chip asked.

"Don't be impertinent. Though it wouldn't hurt to have someone looking a bit more presidential for a change."

"Regardless of his politics?" Chip said.

She looked at him in the mirror. "If he is a Christian, trust me, his politics will be just fine."

"Watch it!" I cried.

She swerved just in time to miss a pickup parked along the side of the road. And the camper in front of it.

"What are they doing here?" I asked.

She slowed and turned into my driveway. "The pickup is new. The camper arrived yesterday."

"Because . . . ?"

A chunky man in a uniform, that fit ten or fifteen pounds ago, appeared in front of us. She brought the car to a stop.

"Who is this guy?" I demanded as he stepped forward and peered inside. "What's going on?"

Once satisfied, he motioned us forward. Patricia nodded and we continued down the driveway. "Darlene's idea," she said. "With so many kooks showing up, she thought it would be good to hire security."

I turned to look out the back window. "They're here to see me?"

"They usually leave when they learn you're not home."

Marveling, I shook my head in silence. She parked the car and we climbed out. The kitchen door flew open and Siggy raced toward me leaping and barking. Good ol' Siggy. Despite his neurosis, he always brought a certain peace to my chaos. Once he finished the greeting—a procedure involving barking, jumping, and muddy paw-prints—he began chasing his tail into oblivion.

Good ol' Siggy.

CHAPTER
TWENTY-ONE

DESPITE AMBER'S PLEAS, Chip did not stick around to watch the Trevor Hunter show that evening. Nor did I. Not because I'd been bumped from the lineup—though I wouldn't put that type of petulance past me—but because I didn't need to be reminded of my digging in and saying no to Yeshua. That didn't stop Amber from watching the show and placing Billie-Jean in front of the screen since, "It's never too soon to expose their little souls to God's truth." Patricia also stuck around, though I suspect it had more to do with Trevor's guest for the evening than his teaching.

The following Sunday I was grateful for another one of Darlene's spreads of fried chicken, mashed potatoes and gravy, cornbread, collards, and her usual Southern fare. The meals were becoming a tradition. One even Patricia felt comfortable enough to occasionally join. But this Sunday someone was missing.

"Chip's not coming?" Darlene asked as we took our seats.

Amber shook her head.

"But free meals are his specialty."

"We're uh," Amber's voice thickened. "We're taking some time off."

The table grew silent. A surprising phenomena considering the participants.

"What did he do this time?" Darlene asked.

Amber looked down, hair covering her face.

Patricia reached out to her hand, "Ambrosia?"

She looked up, mascara streaming from her eyes.

"Oh, honey," Darlene took her other hand. "What's wrong. You can tell me." Amber shook her head. Darlene continued, "We're here for you, you know that. Sweetie?"

Finally, after a hearty sniff, she mumbled, "He's doing weed again."

I blinked, not even knowing marijuana had been an issue (another testimony to my outstanding skills as her guardian). To my defense I said, "Not around the baby. He never smoked around the—"

"Gummies," Darlene interrupted.

"Candy?" I asked.

"Welcome to the twenty-first century, Grandpa."

Amber gave another sniff. "And now he wants to have sex. Even though we haven't, I mean not since we learned it's a sin."

"Men are dogs," Darlene said.

I had no defense.

Amber pulled back her hands and swiped her nose. "He thinks I'm being stupid."

"Chip said that?" I asked. The kid could be irritating, but never rude, especially around Amber and the baby. Despite all his flaws it was clear he treasured both.

Amber shook her head. "No. He says, he says he doesn't want to stumble me, whatever that means. He thinks it's good I still believe in the Bible. He's just . . . he says he's outgrown it; he doesn't want to be a bad influence on me."

"But having sex with you is okay," Patricia said.

Amber sniffed. "He's got needs."

"Dogs," Darlene repeated.

Patricia chose her words more carefully. "So . . . Chip was a Christian and now he's not?"

She swallowed. "He's into truth, not hypocrisy."

"And this all happened since we got back?" I asked.

Another nod.

Unable to resist a good jab, Darlene quoted, *"And the truth shall make you free."*

ా

The next few weeks were relatively peaceful—if you discount the occasional car parked outside my driveway, having to change my cell number, forgoing church or just about any public gathering, and staying off social media. Nevertheless, the posts and videos just kept growing. Though I considered myself retired, done with the healing business, Darlene said I was blowing up. Something about avoiding public attention makes the public want more—and when they can't get it, they make it up. Even that first fellow I prayed for in my hospital room and whose family couldn't wait to get him out of there, wrote about the deep inspirational talks we used to have.

If you can't trust the internet, who can you trust?

Amber spent much of the time in her room. When she did show her face, it was often drawn and tear-streaked. Nothing hurts like teen heartbreak . . . unless it's losing your first love. Amber suffered both. And, as much as I hate to admit it, I missed the highs and lows of her emotional schizophrenia. I even found myself clowning around or playing the fool (some things come naturally) just to make her smile.

More often than not, it was received with a scornful shake of the head, but when I succeeded, it made me feel a little lighter. Strange, after all my complaints about a life turned upside down, I was just a bit happier when she was happy, and just a bit sadder when she was sad. Like it or not, and doing my best to live in denial, my heart had slowly been captured by a fifteen-year-old.

Naturally, I blamed it all on Chip—when I wasn't blaming Trevor—when I wasn't blaming myself (some things just come naturally). But there was more to it than Amber and Chip. How many others—teens and adults—were being confused by Trevor Hunter's lifestyle and "half-gospel"?

It had been a while since I last saw Yeshua, which may have been my doing, or his—I'll let the theologians figure that out. Either way, I was both excited and nervous when he finally showed up—this time in a dream.

CHAPTER
TWENTY-TWO

YESHUA WORE A white tuxedo glimmering in blinding light. He danced slowly with a bride whose back remained to me. Her white gown shimmered in the same light and was made of flowing chiffon with beaded lace and draped sleeves. Below their feet lay the utter blackness of outer space, punctuated by bright stars and swirling galaxies. And surrounding them were the same chords I heard in heaven—ethereal voices mixing and drifting in and out of one another. I stood watching with the other Yeshua, the one wearing his trademark robe and sandals.

"Is this . . . this is a dream, right?" I asked.

He gave one of his wry smiles. "That's one explanation."

"Okay. . ." I said. "If it's not a dream, where exactly are we?"

"Eternity."

"Eternity? Like in the future?

"And the present."

"The present and the future?

"And the past."

"All three?"

His smile broadened. "Which is why it's called eternity."

"Alright . . ." I said. "And I suppose there's some important symbolism in all this?" Before he could respond, I gave the answer, "Which you'll give me the opportunity to figure out."

He broke into a grin. "You really are getting the hang of this."

I shook my head and finally got down to the real issue. "Look, about saying no to you. I really feel bad about that."

"No, you feel guilty."

"There's a difference?"

"Feeling bad is conviction; that's from me. Feeling guilty is from the parasite."

I frowned, figuring this was another concept that would take time to unpack. I tried a different approach. "Darlene says I'm still viral, blowing up all over the internet."

"Absence makes the heart grow fonder."

"Patricia says it was all the work of the devil."

He said nothing, continuing to watch the dancing couple.

"You can see her point, right? I mean the Bible never talks about resurrecting college kids off the streets or breaking into hospitals to heal babies."

"It never mentions toasters, lawn mowers, or TVs either. Would you call them the works of the devil?"

"Well, no, but—"

"Except maybe TV. Some of those shows." He shook his head. "And we thought the Roman Colosseum was dehumanizing."

I scowled, then looked back to the couple. "Can you at least tell me who she is? The bride?"

"Trevor."

I smirked. "Trevor Hunter? In a bridal gown?"

"Is that a problem?"

"Well, no, I mean if that's his thing."

"Over a dozen times in Scripture I call you my Bride. Not my servant, not my companion, not even my wife. I speak about you with the same intimacy as a groom for his bride on their wedding night."

I may have shifted uncomfortably, I'm not sure.

He continued, "When I speak of us knowing one another I use that same word 'know' to describe the sexual relations between a man and a woman."

"Like—" I cleared my throat, "Adam knowing Eve?"

"'And the two shall become one flesh.'"

"That's, uh . . . *intimate*."

"That's my passion for you, Will. Not the sexual intercourse of flesh, but the deeper intercourse of spirit."

This time I know I shifted uncomfortably. I focused back on the couple. "But there's more you want to show me, isn't there."

He smiled, this time sadly. "You are getting good at this." As he spoke the couple began turning and I finally caught a glimpse of Trevor's face. In the bright light it glistened with moisture. But not from tears. As he continued turning, I saw it was covered in large, grotesque boils. Some were broken and oozing. Others bleeding. And mixed with the blood and ooze was something like smeared dirt and mud.

"What's wrong with him?" I cried.

Yeshua said nothing.

"That's not Trevor," I said. "That's how you see his organization, right? The waste, the lavish excess."

"No." He softly replied. "That's how I see him."

"Because of the sex? The hypocrisy?"

"And many things you need not know."

"I thought you loved everybody."

"I do."

"Then . . ."

"He refuses to repent. We've pleaded with him, time after time. But he refuses."

I pointed to Trevor, his hideous face. "And this . . ."

"By refusing the Spirit's power to repent, he is destroying his identity."

"I thought the problem was . . . you said his problem was doing things his way instead of yours. 'Step Three,' you called it."

"Yes. And by doing my work the world's way, he turns to the world's pleasures to relieve its pressure."

"Through adultery."

"And things you need not know," he repeated.

We continued watching, but even now I understood the bottom line. I knew where this was leading. "You still want me to tell him."

"He needs to be warned."

"You're giving me another chance?"

"That's what grace does."

"But . . . who am I? I'm a nobody."

"You're his brother."

I blew out a breath of frustration. "Earlier, back at the beginning when I wanted to judge him, you told me to stand down. You said his way was better than mine."

"I did."

"And now? Now that I don't want to?"

"Now is the time you should."

"That makes no sense!"

"Now you'll be acting in my love. Not your self-righteousness."

"So you want me to call him out."

"No, Will. I want you to call him up. To his true identity."

"And if I don't?"

He remained silent.

"If I keep saying no?"

He looked down, then sadly shook his head.

"What?"

Quietly, he answered, "You don't want to see this."

"Humor me."

He raised his eyes to mine; they were moist with compassion. But I had no intention of backing down. When he saw that, he nodded toward the dancing couple. I watched as Trevor, the bride, pulled away from Yeshua, the groom. Yeshua reached for him, but Trevor stepped back, looking away, refusing to meet his gaze. Then, without a word, he turned and walked away. Yeshua beckoned him to return but he continued walking.

A breeze stirred. I felt nothing, but saw it brushing against Trevor's hair, the draped sleeves of his gown. The surrounding air filled with a faint, yellow haze. He began to cough. I smelled only a faint odor of sulfur, but watched as he put his hand over his nose and mouth trying not to gag. The wind grew stronger, tugging at the folds of his gown.

Somehow, without walking, Yeshua and I followed. With every step Trevor took, the wind blew harder. He lowered his head, fighting to keep his balance as the wind quickly grew to gale force, then hurricane. One of the gown's flapping sleeves began to rip, then tore off flying into the storm. The second followed. Seams began splitting. Pieces ripped apart, sailing away, one after another, until his body was barely covered in tattered strips of cloth, whipping and snapping. Over the roaring wind, the singing turned to moans, then screams, then shrieks.

I spun to Yeshua and shouted, "Where are we? What is this place?"

There was no answer save the tears spilling onto his face. The yellow haze darkened to orange then red. That's when I saw the flames. Below us, above us. On every side. But they gave off no heat. At least to us.

"AUHHH!"

I turned back to Trevor. The remaining pieces of gown had caught fire. The flames raced across them and his body, igniting both, engulfing both.

"NO!" He staggered and fell to his knees, throwing his head from side to side like a tortured animal—as his flesh caught fire, beginning to bubble. "NO!" Charring and turning black. "NO!"

"Do something!" I yelled.

Yeshua simply watched, his face racked with grief.

"Help him!"

He shook his head. "Free will!" he shouted over the wind. "His choice! Not mine!"

"That's impossible!" I turned back to Trevor. His entire body was on fire; charred and molten flesh falling away. Then, to my astonishment, he raised a burning hand

and shoved it into his mouth. He bit down hard on the flaming fingers, screaming in pain as he tore them from his hand, knuckles and bones snapping and cracking. He began to chew. I watched in horror as he ate his own body, swallowing, shoving more into his mouth—screaming in pain as he tore and chewed and swallowed, chewed and swallowed.

I spun back to Yeshua. "Look at him! LOOK!"

Yeshua nodded, his face wet with tears.

I spun back to Trevor. With one flaming hand and the burning stub of the other, he reached down to his thigh and tore away the last of the burning gown. He opened his mouth, and howling, sank his teeth deep into the burning flesh.

"What is he doing?" I cried. "What is he doing!?"

"Eating!"

"WHAT!?"

"He no longer feeds upon me, but himself!"

I could find no words. Other cries surrounded us.

"Free will?" I shouted. "He brought this on himself?"

"Not only him!"

"What?"

Yeshua motioned behind us. I turned to see Jordan, her own body on fire, chewing on her own flesh. And behind her? Thousands, tens of thousands, mostly young, approaching from behind—their clothes also on fire, many crawling, some already eating parts of their bodies, screaming in anguish.

"Who are they?" I shouted. "What are they doing?"

"Following him to hell!"

CHAPTER
TWENTY-THREE

HELL? LIKE SCROOGE and the Ghost of Christmas Future I wasn't sure if I'd seen what *might* be, or that *would* be. Either way I'd never been so terrified.

Hell? During all his visits Yeshua never once brought up the subject. Yet, according to Google, the supreme source of all knowledge and wisdom, of the 1,900 verses he spoke in the Gospels, nearly sixty referred to hell or hades or whatever it's called (I still don't know the difference). Sixty. How was that possible? And the look on his face when we were there, if there was where we were—I'd never seen him filled with such grief.

So I wasn't entirely surprised when Trevor's people found my new number and asked me to fly down and join his prayer team in Las Vegas. I didn't exactly know what that meant, but after the dream and seeing Yeshua's passion and Trevor's anguish, how could I refuse? Of course this won me no friends with the grown-ups—Patricia, sure I was selling out the gospel, Darlene sure I was just selling it.

With Chip out of the picture and Amber staying with Billie-Jean, I traveled solo—just me and my Uber driver, with his overabundance of pine air freshener, to Sea-Tac. This was followed by the four-hour-and-twenty-minute delay due to bad weather, and the two-and-half-hour, white-knuckler to Harry Reid International Airport. Yet, despite all that time and prayer (I did mention the white-knuckler, yes?), I still had little idea how to broach the subject with Trevor Hunter, the Gen Z, Christian superstar.

I asked Yeshua for insight but, never a fan of enabling me, he remained silent. I only had his past teaching and my earlier visits to those Bible Hall-of-Famers—which was like comparing major league players to a minor league player (or, in my case, little league).

After making my way through the terminal with slot machines at nearly every available location (except the restroom), I met Pug at baggage claim. "Hey, dude, glad you could make it." He shook my hand, pulling me into another one of those jock-man half-hugs. I explained I only had a carry-on (Amber did not help me pack) and we headed off to an ultra-luxurious, white limousine. I'd never seen a stretch limo except in movies and was unsure which of the six doors to open.

Once inside, I was met with a leather, turquoise-colored seat wrapping around the cabin. Other than a heavily-tinted window filling one wall, the only light came from the built-in crystal chandelier in the roof and the ruby-red tracer lights in the floor—pulsing to the beat of, what else, Bob Marley.

"Pretty fancy," I said.

"How's that?"

"All this for some prayer supporter."

"Haven't you heard?" He was already typing on his phone.

"Heard?"

"With the sucky weather, we had to switch things up."

"Switch things up?"

"Great news. I'll let Trev tell you." Staring at the phone he shouted, "What!?"

I tried again. "You said, 'switch things up'?"

"Yeah." He resumed typing, his thumbs a blur.

"What kind of—"

"Listen dude, not trying to be rude, but with all the delays I got fires to put out." He motioned to the mirrored bar up front, its sink stocked with ice. Beside it was a lit, mini-wine cellar. A drink was the first thing I needed, and the last thing I'd choose. At least until I had some details. I sat back in the plush seat and pretended to relax while praying my usual mantra: *Now what are you doing?*

The ride to town was short, the topography flat, except for the distant mountains to the west and the billboards. I counted at least three advertising accidental claim lawyers. Soon we were on the Strip—an amazing cacophony of palm trees, monster hotels, and sections of street impersonating New York City (with a half-scale Statue of Liberty), Paris, (with a sparkling Eiffel Tower), Venice (with its canals), a pyramid (with illuminated sphinx), and a massive globe with wandering, cartoon eyes. Everything was about flashing lights and dazzling color, including the giant video screens towering above, displaying every imaginable product, person, and yes, persuasion. The sidewalk swarmed with moms and dads in cargo pants and flip-flops, children in tennis shoes with blinking lights, grandmas in sunhats, and girls in tops so scanty they served as mere accessories.

Pug must have seen my open mouth because he paused just long enough to say, "Impressed?"

I started to answer but was stopped by the cries. Despite the music and the hum of the limo, I heard screaming. Outside voices shouting, "Feed me! Feed me! Feed me!" And then they were gone, disappearing as quickly as they appeared.

"Dude?" Pug asked, "you good?"

I blinked. "Yeah, uh . . ."

"Cool, cause here's the best for last." He motioned to the window as the giant Cube came into view. On its closest panel was a 50 x 70-foot video of the grinning Trevor Hunter. While, swirling above his head in bright green florescent letters, were the words: "Celebrate You!"

Pug chuckled. "Not bad, huh?"

I could find no answer.

"And check out the crowd."

Below the Cube, stretching down the street and out of sight, was a line of people, mostly young.

Pug grinned. "And the doors won't open for two more hours."

We pulled around the Cube, its second panel showing an ocean beach with Trevor's arms draped around Jordan and daughter, London. All three were laughing as the words "Celebrate You!" circled above their heads.

The limo turned into a gated area and pulled to a stop in front of large, cargo bay doors. Beside it a smaller one was marked VIP.

"Here we are," Pug said. He opened the limo door and stepped outside. Turning back to me, he called, "Awesome! At least he's here on time."

I followed Pug out into the hot, desert air. Not thirty feet away I saw the dark cloud Chip and I had seen in Malibu. Now that it wasn't moving it looked more like the gathering of black smudges which had hovered over the accident near Patricia's church. From its center, stepping out of his own white limo, was Governor Robert Proctor.

"Governor!" Pug called.

Proctor looked up from his iPad and grinned, "Pug!"

Pug started to him and motioned for me to follow. I hesitated, not anxious to enter the cloud.

"How was your flight?" Pug asked.

"Rock and roll, baby."

Pug laughed as they shook hands. "Yeah, weather's messin' with everything." He turned and motioned for me to join them. "This here is—"

"I know," Proctor flashed me a dazzling-white grin. "Will Thomas, the Miracle Man." I was shocked he knew me. "Come to help us make a little history, have you?"

"Uh . . ." I threw a look to Pug who was too busy impressing the governor to respond.

But Proctor wasn't finished. "Thanks for stepping in. I really appreciate it."

CHAPTER
TWENTY-FOUR

"HEY JORDAN," PUG called over to the stage, "where's boss man?"

"Topside," she said.

"Cool. Oh, and Proctor's here."

"He is? Terrific!" Shielding her eyes from the lights, Jordan looked up to the crew atop the scaffolding who were making last-minute lighting adjustments. "You guys don't need me anymore, do you?"

"We're good," a voice called from the darkness.

With that, Jordan dashed across the stage with all the excitement of a giddy, high school girl.

Pug chuckled. "Jordan and Proctor, they got what you'd call a new and personal arrangement."

I frowned. "Arrangement?"

He gave me a wink. "Don't ask, don't tell. Right, bro?"

We walked to the stage. Surrounding us were four giant walls, stretching out then coming together at the very top. The bottom half of each wall was filled with seats, while the second half stretched high overhead in four, enormous, projection screens that came together at the apex.

Pug grinned. "Epic, right?" An obvious understatement. "And the whole top opens; that's where Jesus drops in."

I could only stare.

We reached a door on the other side of the stage. It opened to a black, girder stairway, like an interior fire escape, stretching at least seven stories above us.

"We're going up there?" I asked.

He nodded and started the climb. "You good?"

"No problem." It was an obvious lie that became apparent by the half-way mark. After a moment to catch my breath (and pray there was a defibrillator nearby), we continued. Eventually we reached the top and another door. Pug pushed it open and we stepped outside onto a catwalk. Trevor stood at the railing twenty feet away looking down at the crowd.

"Hey, Trev," Pug shouted over the breeze, "got the man here, himself."

Trevor looked over and called, "Hey, Will."

I started toward him, gripping the railing a bit too tightly. Heights and I were never great friends. It wasn't the fear of falling that worried me; it was the abrupt stop. Once I arrived, Trevor gave me another one of those macho, pull-me-into-a-half-hug things. "Thanks for coming, man."

"You world-builders, do your thing," Pug called, turning to leave. "I got a ton of crap to sort out."

Trevor nodded, "Later."

Pug disappeared through the door, leaving the two of us alone, seventy feet above Las Vegas.

"Quite a view, huh?"

I nodded, doing my best not to look down.

"Pug tell you the good news?"

"I saw the governor showing up."

Trevor laughed. "Oh, he's more than showing up." He motioned below to a parking lot. I stole a look quick enough to see a dozen vehicles, mostly vans—some with microwave towers, others with satellite dishes. Printed on their sides were letters and logos: CBS, CNN, FOX NEWS. I didn't bother to check the others.

"Impressive," I said.

He laughed. "Right. But don't think they came to see me. Well, not yet. No, my friend. Tonight, right here, in less than two hours, Governor Robert Proctor will be announcing his bid to run for president."

I turned to him, stunned. "Here?"

"Not bad, huh?"

I probably nodded—I don't remember.

"And you, pal, with all the flight delays and cancellations, who do you suppose will be opening all this up in prayer?"

I scowled, bracing for the worst.

He gave another laugh. "You, my friend. Dr. Will Thomas, the Miracle Man."

I gripped the railing a little tighter.

"How cool is that?" he said. "I told you I wouldn't forget, and here you are. You'll be giving the invocation. That's right. Will Thomas will no longer be some semi-obscure miracle worker; he's about to become a household name."

I had no words which made sense because I had no thoughts.

He slapped me on the shoulder. "Not bad, huh?" He paused, letting the news sink in. Finally, he said, "So what do you say?"

I swallowed—which was a stupid thing to do because I had nothing to swallow. I noticed a bird working the currents above us. I watched as it came closer, then swooped in and landed on the railing not three feet from Trevor. A dove. Trevor hadn't noticed but, of course, I did.

"So what does the Miracle Man have to say about all that?"

I took another swallow, just as futile as the first.

"Well?"

After a deep breath, and a quick glance to the dove, I gave my answer, "Uh . . . no." Disappointed my voice was an octave higher than normal, I tried again. "Thank you, Trevor. I appreciate the offer, what you're trying to do, but, uh, I have to pass."

"I'm sorry?" he said.

"I can't."

"You can't?"

I cleared my throat. "I . . . won't."

"What? You know what I'm asking, right? The opportunity I'm giving you?"

I looked back to the dove. He cocked his head at me. I wasn't sure what that meant but knew it was now or never. "I do," I said. "And I appreciate it, but—" With another breath, I pressed on. "But do you understand, what you're doing?" Trevor frowned. I tried again. "Here, I mean?" More frowning. "You started off with great intentions. Like we talked about in your office. But . . . what I'm trying to say is . . ."

"Say it, Will. What's going on?"

"I believe, in my opinion . . ." I paused.

"Waiting here."

"In my opinion you could give a better representation of the gospel."

He laughed. "I could what?"

"You're telling everybody they're good and they're loved and they're special, which is okay but . . ."

"But?"

"It's not true."

"Excuse me?"

"We're loved and we're special, no argument there. But we're not good. Not until—" I took another breath.

"Not until we confess our sins and ask Jesus to clean us."
I cringed at what sounded like a religious bromide, but
knew it wasn't. "Jesus paid for our sins. But we have to
give them to him. He won't just come and take them
against our will. We have to confess them first. We have
to ask."

To my relief, Trevor didn't break into fits of laughter.
He just looked down at the street.

Encouraged, I continued. "I mean, isn't that what you
used to teach? When you were starting out?"

He remained silent.

"That's what you said. In your office. Remember?"

Another moment before he answered. "You know,
you're not the first to say that. People hit me with that sort
of thing all the time."

"And?"

"I tell them, maybe it's time for a newer version.
Because the old sure isn't working." He nodded to the line
of young people stretching below us. "Look at them, Will.
Do you think they want to be told they're sinners?"

"I know," I sighed. "I know. But they have to admit
they're sick before a doctor can cure them. You said it yourself, you're only preaching half the gospel. The grace half.
They need to hear the other half too, the truth half."

"That we're all sinners and going to hell?"

"That we're all sinners who need Jesus to save us from
hell."

He motioned back to the crowd. "These kids. Look at them. Look how many are coming to God."

I shook my head. "No."

"No?"

"They're . . . coming to you."

I saw the muscles in his neck stiffen. I understood. I was surprised at my own boldness.

"So . . . what are you saying? That you won't do the invocation? That you won't do the prayer because I'm only preaching 'half the gospel'?"

I knew there was more. I knew if I really loved Trevor, or Yeshua for that matter, I'd have to say the rest. I glanced at the dove who stopped preening his feathers and looked at me. I went for broke. "It's not just that."

Trevor turned to me, waiting.

"It's because of the sin in your organization. And—in your own life."

"Whoa, whoa, whoa."

"You're sleeping with Cheri, Trev."

"That's none of—"

"Your wife is having an affair with the governor of California. Your daughter sleeps with whoever she—"

"Keep my family out of this!"

"But it's the same thing, don't you see? Your personal life spills out all over your message. Or maybe it's the other way around. Maybe it's your message that's spilling out all over—"

"Who the hell are you to judge me?"

"I'm a nobody."

"You can say that again. Divorced, jobless. And talk about reputation."

"Yes. Yes. And if it wasn't for Jesus, I'd—"

"You're no better than me."

"Probably worse. That's what I'm trying to—"

"So stay out of my face. I don't need you preaching at me."

"But you do. God wants me to tell you—"

"If God's got something to say, he'll say it."

"He has been. Over and over again."

Trevor looked back to the crowd.

I continued. "Those kids, they're too valuable for you and Jordan to keep doing what you're doing. You and Jordan are too valuable. That's why I'm here. And if you won't listen to his love—"

"Love? You call this love?"

"If you won't listen to his love, he'll find another—"

"Alright, fine. You don't want to pray, don't pray. You want to live your little life in obscurity, be my guest. But keep my family and my personal life out of this." He shook his head. "I was trying to do you a favor, man. Give you a leg up on the competition—"

"It's not a compet—"

"But if you don't want it, fine."

"It's not that I don't—"

"Right. Whatever." He checked his watch. "Listen, we got seventy minutes before curtain. I need time to clear my head. 'Specially with this little download of yours."

"Trev—"

"If you change your mind, let Pug know. If not . . ." He saw no need to finish.

"Trevor, I just—"

"You need to leave, okay."

"Trev—"

"Go."

I stood, hesitating.

"What? Do I have to call security?"

"No, of course not."

"Then go." He looked back at the crowd.

I waited. When it was clear we were finished, I turned and started across the catwalk. Once at the door, I looked back a final time. He remained staring down at the crowd. Only then did I notice the dove was gone. I didn't see him or hear him fly away. He was just gone.

CHAPTER
TWENTY-FIVE

AFTER A FEW wrong turns, I found my way out of the Cube. The doors had just opened and I began my walk past the endless line of ticket holders. I was headed to catch the monorail train for Hotel Opulence, "The newest and best in all Vegas," which Pug booked for us; why was I not surprised. My flight would be first thing in the morning and it couldn't come soon enough.

As I walked, Yeshua joined me. "Thank you, Will," he said. "That was a good thing you did."

"If it was so good, how come I feel so bad?"

"Love can be hard."

I glanced down. The shiny scar tissue in his hands said he knew what he was talking about. We continued down the line of attendees: mostly late teens to early thirties— stocking hats, shaved heads, man-buns, dreadlocks, beards, jeans, frilly dresses, T-shirts—of every race imaginable.

"So many," I said.

"It's only the—" he cleared the catch in his throat. "It's only the beginning."

I looked to him. "He's not going to stop, is he?" I asked. "He's just going to keep going."

Yeshua answered softly, "Fame's a powerful opiate."

"But I did all I could, right?"

"You did a brave thing, Will."

I frowned. Not that I was expecting flowers and accolades, but there was something in his voice. "You didn't—you didn't expect me to do the invocation, did you?"

He remained silent.

"That's not my thing, you know that. I don't pray out loud."

He nodded. "Except for old men in hospitals."

"That's entirely different."

We were interrupted by one of the kids. "Hey! Aren't you that mystery miracle man?"

Others in the line turned to look. I shook my head.

"No, you are," another said. "It *is* you."

"Sorry," I said, "wrong guy," and continued walking. I stole an uneasy look to Yeshua. He was so preoccupied watching each individual, I doubted he heard me. And his expression—I'd only seen a sorrow that deep twice. Once when he was on the cross looking down at me, and more recently in my dream.

We walked in silence to the monorail station, but not before passing a dumpster diver rummaging through the garbage behind a bar and grill. A flashing LED sign read,

The Sin Pit. The Sin Pit. The Sin Pit. In earlier times I might have thought the name clever. But now . . .

As we started up the stairs to the train's platform, I noticed Yeshua moving slower, his steps heavier. We reached the top which was packed and swarming with tourists. A girl in a silver mini skirt, not much older than Amber, and with the same penchant for mascara, slinked up to me. I knew what she had in mind and shook my head before she asked. Without a word, she turned to find another customer, wobbling slightly, an apparent novice to high heels. I chose not to look at Yeshua.

It wasn't until the train pulled to a stop and we boarded that I repeated my question. "What more could I do?"

"You did well, Will." His voice was thick. "I'm proud of you."

"But. You were hoping for . . . ?" I finally looked to him. His eyes were wet with moisture and he shook his head.

"No," I insisted, "tell me."

We made our way through the crowd and found a seat. As the train started forward, I pressed him again. "Tell me."

When it was clear I wouldn't relent, he quietly answered, "The cost is too great."

"Meaning? What cost?"

"You'd have to give up your life."

"I did that once. In the prison, remember?"

He nodded, watching each of the passengers. "This time it would be greater."

"Greater than dying?" There was a commotion in the center of the car hidden by the crowd. "You wanted me to pray, is that it? Even though you hate what he's doing, you wanted me to pray."

"I pray for everyone."

I sighed in heavy frustration.

He swallowed, his voice thicker as he repeated a phrase he'd used before. "Wheels turning within wheels. In praying, you would join the great heroes of faith."

"Yeah, right," I scoffed. "Like in the Bible."

He turned to me, eyes swollen with emotion. "You are in the Bible."

I blinked, searched his face for irony. There was none.

The crowd cheered and began to part, giving room to a young man, his face in heavy makeup. He wore gold, sequined hot pants and a halter top. He was sliding up and down one of the poles, spinning around it, kissing and licking it, rubbing his body against it, for all intents and purposes pole dancing. The crowd clapped, some cheered, encouraging him to grow more and more obscene. I turned to Yeshua just in time to see a tear spill onto his cheek. I looked back to the dancer. Only now he wasn't a man. Now, I saw what Yeshua saw . . . a little boy, six or seven, desperate for the crowd's love.

I felt Yeshua shudder. I turned to see him leaning over. I began hearing other voices—the ones I heard while riding in the limo.

"Feed me. Feed me. Feed me."

I looked back to the crowd on the train. Only now they weren't tourists; now they were starving, emaciated bodies. Skin stretched over bone, screaming:

"Feed me! Feed me! Feed me!"

I stared, dumbfounded. Their appearance changed again—morphing into a crowd of first-century peasants. They stood in bright sunlight on a dusty road leading to the city I'd come to recognize as Jerusalem. I stood beside Yeshua as they cried to him:

"Hosanna! Hosanna! Hosanna!"

Face wet with tears, unable to stand, he sank to the road. He convulsed in a sob, then another—as the crowd kept shouting, a mixture of what we heard on the train and what we heard on the hill:

"Hosanna Feed Hosanna Me Hosanna . . ."

I stooped down, trying somehow to comfort him. But he'd have none of it. Instead, finding strength, he raised his head and cried out to the people, "If you only knew this day what would bring you peace! But now," he gasped a ragged breath. "Now it is hidden from your eyes!"

The peasants stood in confusion. Or unbelief. Or both. I felt the train begin to slow. Their faces blurred, returning to those of the tourists. Yeshua remained beside me, hunched over, his body trembling in silent sobs. As we rolled to a stop, I knew what had to be done. My own eyes stung with moisture as I reached for his arm. I tried pulling him with me to his feet. But he was too spent.

"Come on," I choked, "we can do this."

He turned to me with those dreadful, mournful eyes.

I pulled again. With effort the two of us rose.

"Okay," I whispered. "Let's get off this thing." He nodded and we started forward. He leaned upon me as we pushed our way through the crowd to the open door. We stepped off and the door hissed shut behind us. As the train pulled away, another approached on another track—heading the opposite direction.

"Come on," I repeated.

He straightened himself and the two of us crossed the platform to board it.

CHAPTER
TWENTY-SIX

AS WE APPROACHED the Cube, I saw the cloud again. Not as thick as before but wider, the dark smudges spread out, hovering around the structure in a thin, blotchy fog. I slowed, hesitating, until Yeshua whispered, his voice still hoarse. "For me, Will. For love." I turned but he was gone. Instead, he was replaced by the soldiers in my hospital room and the beach. They surrounded me on all sides—the gnarly warrior with the scar leading the way. As we approached the fog it swirled, pulling back, dissipating like smoke blown away by a fan.

The security guard at the VIP entrance recognized me and opened the door. "You're late," he said. "They're down in the green room."

I thanked him and entered. The fog and my military escort dissolved. But as with Yeshua, I knew they were present. I entered a long, concrete hallway, my footsteps echoing against bare walls. At the far end I heard the audience shouting and calling to each other, everyone anticipating a terrific time. Well, almost everyone.

"What am I supposed to pray?" I whispered. "I don't have anything prepared."

From our heart, Will. Pray from our heart.

"But I'll look like a fool."

And that's stopped you when?

I took certain comfort knowing his humor had returned. I could almost sense a smile. And with that smile, came the assurance. I would know. When it was time, I would know.

Up ahead, I saw Proctor's security agent, a bulldog of a man, posted outside one of the doors. He recognized me and I slowed. "Come for the holy huddle?" he asked, not hiding the smirk in his voice. Before I could answer he shook his head and stepped aside. I opened the door to a large room. The oak floor was polished to a shine with plush throw rugs and leather sofas and chairs scattered throughout. On one wall a giant mirror rose to the fourteen-foot ceiling. The other walls displayed larger-than-life murals of famous performers.

Trever, Jordan, Pug, Cheri, and two dozen staff members, along with Governor Proctor, had formed a circle and were holding hands praying. I stepped silently inside. But Proctor, as if sensing my presence, looked up and grinned. But it wasn't Proctor. Or maybe it was. Either way, for a millisecond, his face flickered into one of those amphibian-face things. And then it was Proctor again.

Unnerved, I slowed, then forced myself to continue. This wasn't about him. Or me.

The prayer concluded with Trevor calling out, "In the ultimate winner's name, we pray, Amen!" Amens were enthusiastically repeated. "Okay, team," he shouted, "it's showtime." He clapped his hands. "Let's go out there and show them some of that holy love!"

"Alright!" they shouted. "Here we go!" More clapping. "Let's do this thing!"

Spotting me, Trevor broke into a grin. He quickly moved through the crowd, calling out to Pug, "Pug, Pug! Join us, dude!" He arrived, giving me a legitimate hug, longer than normal, like he needed it. "Thanks for coming, man."

Pug joined us. "Didn't think you'd make it," he said.

"Oh, he made it." Trevor slapped me on the shoulder. "'Cause he's a team player, right?"

I looked down.

"Just a little cold feet," he said. "And why not, with 20,000 kids and a national TV audience."

"What do I tell Hagen?" Pug asked. "He's stoked about stepping in."

"Hagen's out. Not when we got the Miracle Man, himself."

"Trevor!" one of the guys from the group shouted.

"Be right there!" Trevor called, then turned back to Pug. "Run down the program with Will, let him know when he's up, where he's seated, and let the stage manager know." Then to me, he said, "Keep it short, right dude? Leave the preaching to me." He laughed, then added, "And positive. Positive's what we're about. Right, Pug?"

"Trevor," the voice called.

"Hang on!" he shouted, then back to me with his final words, "You'll do great, don't worry."

"Okay folks," a young woman in a blue blazer called from the open door. "It's that time. Follow me."

More shouts and clapping as we started for the hall-way. By accident or on purpose, Proctor kept a good distance between us, which was fine with me. As we moved down the hall, Pug gave me the rundown, which I barely heard. Hard to hear much of anything when your heart's jackhammering in your ears. We approached another door. Several of the group peeled off and, continuing down the hall, shouted, "Praise God! Break a leg! Knock 'em dead!"

I started to follow until Pug grabbed me. "Not you, dude. You're sitting on stage with Trev and the celebs."

I looked at him, hoping I'd misunderstood. I hadn't. We passed through the door and stepped onto a large, circular stage. It was recessed about ten feet and completely out of sight of the audience. Pug directed me to one of the chairs setting in a semicircle behind a slender, glass podium. "Just relax, man, you'll nail it."

Before I could disagree, he was gone. To my right sat a beautiful brunette, scant clothing and with enough perfume to pass for a flower shop—or funeral home. "Oh, you're the Miracle Man," she said. "It's such an honor to meet you." She shook my hand, seeing no reason to introduce herself which I figured made her some sort of celebrity.

To my left sat a young man equally good-looking with thick, brooding brows, and a messy, I-don't-care-what-I-look-like hairstyle, which was heavily lacquered to keep looking like he didn't care. This one I'm sure I'd seen on TV. I started to introduce myself but was drowned out by a methodic pounding—even louder than my heart.

We heard the audience join in, clapping to the beat, growing louder and louder. Nearly a minute passed before it suddenly stopped. Then a pause, giving the audience plenty of time to shout as anticipation grew until, finally, the opening theme to *2001: A Space Odyssey* began.

"And away we go," the actor shouted, checking his hair and slumping into the chair to look bored and unimpressed.

The stage gave a little jerk and started to move. The crowd cheered as we rose into the brilliant light. We'd barely stopped before two spotlights from opposite sides hit Trevor bounding to the podium as the crazed crowd went crazier.

"Hello, Las Vegas!" he shouted.

The cheers were deafening.

"Hello, America!"

More cheering.

"Are you ready to party!?"

"Yes!" came the roar.

"To celebrate Jesus!?"

"Yes!"

"And you!?"

The auditorium shook with shouting and pounding feet.

"All right, then. 'Cause the next two hours we're going to have ourselves one big party! You and me . . . and Jesus!"

The cheers grew even louder as he shouted, "Wish you could see what I see, what God sees. 'Cause every one of you is beautiful!" He turned to his left. "Right, Jordan?!"

Jordan appeared in another spotlight, met with similar cheering as she crossed the stage to him. "That's right, Trev! And you and me, and everyone in this house and at home, buckle in 'cause we're going to celebrate you!"

More pounding, shouting, and screaming.

"And," Trevor yelled, "as a little surprise, we have with us a very special guest. It's my great, great honor to introduce you to Mr. Robert Proctor, governor of the State of California!"

Another spotlight appeared, hitting Proctor sitting ten chairs to my right. He briefly rose, waved to the crowd, and gave Trevor and Jordan a little salute.

"And," Trevor shouted, "he's got some very, very cool news for all of us."

More cheers and clapping—for what, they had no idea.

"But before we get going, let's kick things off with a talk to the Man upstairs. Is that cool with you?"

"Yes!" they shouted

"I said, is that cool?"

"YES!"

"And who better to talk to the Boss than—if you haven't seen this guy on social media, you've been living under a rock. He's all over the place, healing people and raising them from the dead." The crowd buzzed. "That's right! My good friend, the Miracle Man himself. Dr. Will Thomas!" Over the shouts and cheers he yelled, "Give it up for Miracle Man!"

A blinding light hit me and I sat stunned. Frozen.

"That's your cue," the brunette to my right shouted through a perma-grin.

I couldn't move.

"Go ahead," the actor yelled. "You're on!" I turned to him. "Go for it!"

Somehow, I managed to rise. Trevor and Jordan waited at the podium, cranking their own grins up to high beam.

"Come on, Doc!" Trevor shouted. "Bring us into the Big Man's presence!"

"Go!" the actor shouted.

I gave the order to my feet and they started moving.

Revving the audience back up again, Trevor shouted, "Let's hear it for Miracle Man! Come on now!"

I glanced off stage. If ever there was a time to turn and run for my life it was now. But the memory of Yeshua on that train, broken and weeping, would not leave me. Would never leave. I turned back to Trevor and Jordan. The chains I saw in Trevor's office had returned, wrapping around the arms and legs of both himself and his wife. And surrounding the podium—floating on both sides as well as above and below, were the frog-like creatures—the gargoyles with bulging eyes and fangs, shrieking and hissing. As I continued forward, their spindly arms and razor-sharp talons reached for me, creating a deadly passageway as they had in Malibu. No, not a passageway. This time, more clearly, I saw. It was a mouth. And it was widening. Waiting for me. Above it hovered a black, shiny snout with flaring nostrils. And above that, yellow pupils slit vertically like a snake's. Its long tail stretched into the audience, whipping back and forth.

I had to stop. But I wouldn't. Because of Yeshua. Because of his passion for the kids—and for Trevor and Jordan. My legs were rubber, they had no feeling. I heard nothing but my pounding heart and the hissing shrieks as I stepped forward and entered the serpent's gaping maw.

TWENTY-SEVEN

THE MOUTH CONTINUED to widen, but not on its own accord. It was the soldiers' swords. They appeared midair, hacking and slicing off pieces of the surrounding creatures. With every step I took, the swords cut more away—whirling and slashing, amputating and decapitating—the things pulling back, shrieking and wailing. My action, my faith, was the catalyst, but the swords were the weapons, driving the remaining creatures further and further from me. They were still present, but too far away to be a threat. Now the only enemy was my own fear.

I arrived at the podium, gripping its edges for support. I squinted past the lights to the cheering crowd.

Okay, if you got something, I prayed, *now would be good.*

Yeshua remained quiet.

Any time.

Still nothing.

For a moment, my silence quieted the crowd. But as I kept waiting, they began to stir. Trevor fidgeted. And still I waited. What did Yeshua say about rushing ahead—jumping in and doing his will my way? Not this time. This time I waited.

Trevor laughed and turned to the crowd. "It's going to be good, guys. He's just waiting to hear from the Man himself. Right, Will?"

That's when I noticed the dove. I watched as he circled the auditorium once before diving toward me. I turned my head, bracing for impact but he slowed, fluttering his wings, before gently landing on my shoulder. I glanced to Trevor and Jordan. They didn't see him. But he was there. And with his presence I felt the power I first felt in my hospital room. I breathed deeply, feeling it rush into my body, my mind settling, my fear dissolving. I looked down at my hands. Their trembling slowed. I still had no words, but thoughts began to form and take shape. I knew all I had to do was open my mouth and they would solidify into words.

I bowed my head and began to speak: "Father . . ." The crowd grew quiet. "I know each of us here is your favorite child. Because you're infinite, that's no problem. And I know you loved each of us more than your own Son's life."

"Amen," Trevor said, Jordan echoing him.

"But I know we've failed you, Lord. I know each of us are sinners who have failed."

Trevor cleared his throat.

"But sinners, who you love and who, despite our filth, you desperately want to clean so we can be in your presence . . . forever."

"Yes," Trevor joined in. "Thanks for a love that made the goodness we can celebrate tonight."

I paused, not wanting it to become dueling prayers, hoping to find some common ground. I tried again: "A goodness that can only happen when we admit our failures and give you permission to come inside to clean and to—"

"What he means to say—" I opened my eyes to see Trevor addressing the crowd. "We all have God inside us. We just have to admit and celebrate that goodness." He turned to me. "Right, Will?"

We held each other's gaze until I slowly shook my head. "No," I said. "If you don't let God clean you, your goodness, even at your best is like . . ." I hesitated but these were Yeshua's words not mine. "You're very best is like menstrual rags."

The audience barely had time to murmur before Trevor broke in. "Whoa, partner. I gotta stop you there."

"That's the truth, Trevor. No matter how hard we try, you know we're not good enough on our own to—"

"No, my friend. What I *do* know is you've been working awfully hard lately, to the point of exhaustion." Turning to the audience, he continued, "And I know I probably shouldn't have let you talk me into praying for us tonight. But he's such a fan of ours, it's hard to say no."

He stepped up to me. "I want to personally thank you for giving it a shot. He's a real trooper, folks." He threw his arm around my shoulder and shouted, "So, give it up for Will Thomas, everybody! Give it up for Miracle Man!" The audience clapped. "Kudos to him, right?" More applause. "Am I right?" Some cheered. "So head on back to your seat, Will. Get some rest and enjoy the show because we're here to celebrate the you God has made. Am I right!"

More shouts and applause. I turned, my heart pounding. At first I was unable to even find my chair. Spotting it, I started off and arrived. My face on fire and ears burning, I sat and stared hard at the floor.

I felt a hand on my shoulder then heard Yeshua's gentle voice. "Thank you, brother."

Brother? The word surprised me. I craned my head to look up at him. His eyes were closed, fighting back emotion. But I could tell he was feeling something more—something greater than just gratitude.

What now? I thought. He turned his face from me. Something was up. Growing uneasy, I repeated, *What?*

A shot fired. It sounded like a firecracker. Somebody screamed, "He's got a gun!"

I jerked my head to the right and saw a kid in a buzz cut and army coat racing at Governor Proctor, his arm raised to fire more shots—until the man nearest Proctor, leaped to his feet and lunged for the boy's arm, causing him to discharge another round high into the air. Proctor was hunched over, holding his shoulder.

"Robert!" a voice at the podium screamed. It was Jordan's. Trevor reached for her, but she broke away, running toward the chaos, running toward Proctor.

Another man jumped to his feet, helping the first tackle the kid to the stage, wrestling for the gun. Panic swept through the auditorium, the audience ducking behind seats, scrambling over each other to get away.

"Robert!" Jordan cried as she arrived. "Robert!" I caught a glimpse of him, trying to sit up to meet her, wincing as she stooped down throwing her arms around him. The scuffle with the boy continued until he managed to free his arm just long enough to fire two more shots at the governor. But Jordan was between them. Her head lurched forward from the first round. To the side from the second. He would have fired more if it were not for the bulldog of a security agent who appeared, shooting three, four, five rounds into his chest.

People screamed, others shouted, "911! Call 911!" as Trevor pushed his way through the crowd to his wife. He arrived, dropping to her body which lay unmoving on the stage. Like everyone else I rose to my feet for a better look. I wished I hadn't. The pooling blood, the missing side of her head, were images I will never forget. But it didn't stop Trevor from pulling her into his arms, crying, "Jordy! Jordy!"

The shooter lay ten feet away, eyes open and lifeless. Blood rapidly spread through his jacket. It was over. Those who wrestled him to the stage shared looks then slowly rose to their feet. The initial panic gave way to cries for security, and an ambulance while, sadly, even now some pulled cell phones from their pockets as a news crew scrambled on stage, pressing in with their own camera.

Only then did Trevor spot me. His face wet with tears. "Will," he choked, "help her!" Those gathered around him turned to me. "Do it!" He began to sob. "Fix this . . . fix her!"

I stood, overwhelmed by the event, even more so by the compassion I felt—until I noticed my hands growing warm. Taking my cue, I started toward them. People stepped aside as Trevor held her, waiting. I arrived and knelt, my hands hot. Jordan was gone, there was no doubt, but my hands were on fire. I stretched them toward her, unsure where to place them amidst all the blood. I chose her chest and was about to lay my hands on it, when I saw the dove overhead. I felt gratitude knowing I wasn't in this alone. But instead of descending, he remained above us, wings whistling softly. I watched, waiting for last-minute direction, until he finally floated down. But to my shock, he did not descend upon Jordan. Instead, he gently landed upon the young killer.

"No," I whispered, "that's not possible."

He remained perched on the boy's chest.

"No."

"She's not moving!" Trevor cried. "Fix her, Will! Fix her!"

I stared in disbelief. The dove, ruffled his feathers and waited.

"Will . . ."

He cocked his head at me. I closed my eyes. This was not happening. He could not possibly want this.

"Will! Do something!"

The dove cooed. I opened my eyes. He remained, waiting.

"Will!"

I paused, looked up to those around me. I motioned for them to help me stand. They hesitated. I nodded and they finally bent to help me to my feet.

"What are you doing?!" Trevor shouted.

I turned toward the kid, paused a final time, then started toward him.

"Will!"

People stepped aside. I arrived and stood, staring down at his lifeless body. His coat saturated in blood. My hands hotter than ever.

"Will!"

I knelt next to him, heard the others murmuring and whispering.

"What are you doing?" Trevor shouted. "What are you doing!?"

I reached out my hands. The dove, having clearly marked the place by where he perched, stretched his wings then flew up and away. I laid my palms over the spot, again closing my eyes.

Trevor screamed, shouted, swore. "WILL!"

The kid jerked once, twice, then coughed and gasped in a breath. Life returned to his eyes and they darted back and forth trying to comprehend.

"WHAT HAVE YOU DONE?" Trevor cried. "WHAT HAVE YOU DONE!?"

One or two bent down to the kid as Trevor continued screaming. With help, I rose and stood, unsure what to do. I stared at the boy who was now fighting to sit up. I looked over to Trevor, to his dead wife, to those unable to console him. Once again, I felt Yeshua's hand on my shoulder. But there was no need to turn to him. I could feel his grief. It was palpable—greater than any in the building.

CHAPTER
TWENTY-EIGHT

CALL IT SHOCK, I'm not sure. Either way I was surprised how quickly we seemed to get out of the Cube and back onto the Strip. I was also amazed no one called us out. I suspect it had to do with keeping our heads down, not to mention the sirens, ER vehicles, and mass pandemonium. Then, of course, there were the giant, overhead LED screens drawing everyone's attention with the constant playing and replaying of the shooting. We walked in silence, neither Yeshua nor I spoke. I'm guessing his thoughts were as heavy as my own and maybe he was as grateful for my company as I was for his.

Finally, he said. "Thank you, Will." I turned to him and he explained. "Few are willing to obey to your depth."

I frowned and looked away, not sure how to respond to praise from God.

He continued, "Which is why, long before your birth, we selected you."

My frown deepened. "My whole life has been a mistake, one after another."

He smiled wistfully. "Some of my greatest friends make the greatest mistakes. Moses, David, Paul. It's not the mistakes I pay attention to. It's the heart. And you've been willing to let our hearts knit together in ways you'll never understand."

I snorted. "Not understanding is my specialty."

He turned to me. Though his eyes were red and puffy, I saw the hint of a twinkle. As before, he raised his hand to my head, "Not this understanding, Will." He lowered it to my chest, "This."

I blew out my breath. "And tonight?" I said. "Wheels within wheels within wheels?" He nodded. "But why Jordan?" I asked. "Can you at least explain that?"

"She's with me now."

"With you?"

"I've taken her home before she could do more damage—to herself or others." My frown returned. He explained, "I love her, Will."

"But . . ."

"Sometimes mercy has to be severe."

I paused, chewing on the thought, almost understanding. "And what about Trevor?" I asked.

Yeshua looked down and repeated more softly, "Severe mercy."

Now I didn't understand. Or maybe I didn't want to. Either way, being the king of self-centeredness (another one of my specialties), I finally got around to asking, "What about—" I was too embarrassed to continue.

"You?" he asked.

I nodded. "Everyone's going to hate me, aren't they?"

He nodded. "From coast to coast. Well, except for Siggy."

I cut him a look. He shrugged.

"You mentioned five steps," I said. "That if I wanted to become all you dreamed for me, it would take five steps."

He nodded. "First you accepted my promise."

"And everyone close to me, they all had a good laugh over it."

"Yes. That was number two. Like Joseph's brothers or Abraham's wife, or my own family—you were ridiculed for stepping out and believing."

"And number three," I said. "Trying to do it my own way. Like Abraham with Hagar, Paul eliminating Christians, Satan's temptation to you."

More quietly, Yeshua added, "And Trevor's attempt to spread my love."

Silence settled back over our conversation.

"And number four," I finally said. "Obedience. Joseph refusing to sleep with Potiphar's wife, Paul repenting and changing teams." He nodded and I continued, "You going to the cross."

"And you confronting Trevor, doing all I asked—even when it made no sense."

"Obedience," I repeated. "That's a tough one."

"Sometimes, yes."

"And five?" I asked. More silence. I turned to him. "You said there were five."

He nodded.

"Will it be as hard as tonight?"

"You'll always have me with you."

It wasn't exactly the answer I was hoping for.

"Our hearts are becoming one, Will. Just as mine with the Father's."

I was beginning to understand what he meant. Well, maybe, just a little. It seemed, all night I'd been feeling what he felt, experiencing what he experienced. Nevertheless, I tried again. "What's the next step? Can you at least give me a hint?"

Suddenly we were off the Strip and in a small, room with a dirt floor, rays of sunlight filtering through a thatched roof. Once my eyes adjusted I realized we were back in prison—Joseph's—where we'd spoken to him before. Only this time he didn't see or hear us. Instead he was on his knees, head down on a wooden pallet. His body shuddering, his face obscured by shadow.

"She begged me," he cried. "Perfumed . . . beautiful. I've been celibate, my whole life, locked in this cell for years, but I refused. I obeyed. I obeyed!" He raised his head, shouting to the roof. "And this is my reward?"

I turned to Yeshua who motioned me to keep listening.

"You promised my brothers would kneel before me. And this? Where are you? *I* was faithful—why aren't you!?"

I whispered to Yeshua. "But the story isn't over."

"He doesn't know that. He doesn't know his obedience will make him the second most powerful man in the world—far beyond what I promised. Not only will his brothers bow down to him, but an entire nation."

"Why!?" Joseph rose to his feet, still shouting. "Why!?"

"But first this?" I asked.

Suddenly, we were blinded by sunlight. We stood on a deserted hill, wind whipping our clothes. Not far away a young man, just a boy, lay on a crude platform of piled stones, his hands and feet tied. An old man, the one I'd seen in Joseph's cell, hobbled back and forth brandishing a dagger, shouting at the sky:

"What do you want? What more do you want?!" He stumbled but continued to pace. "You promised me children! *More than the sands of the earth.* And now you want me to kill him. My only hope. I'll father an entire nation, you said. What type of God are you?!"

I turned to Yeshua. "Abraham."

"And his son, Isaac."

"You promised!" the man bellowed.

Watching in silent admiration, Yeshua explained. "He's obeyed. He's agreed to kill his son, his only hope."

"You promised!" he cried.

"Like Joseph, by obeying, he'll receive so much more than my original promise. He'll not be the father of a single nation, but of many, of all who will ever have faith in me."

I turned back to Abraham, only to discover I stood on another hill, surrounded by a jeering mob. At the center of their hatred was a scene I witnessed far too many times—the bloody sacrifice of Yeshua being tortured to death. But this time his passion-filled eyes did not gaze down upon me. This time his head was raised to heaven as he screamed, "My God, my God, why have you forsaken me!"

I turned to the Yeshua beside me. He'd looked way, the memory still taking its toll. "Because of your obedience?" I asked.

"Satan promised I could rule the world. But because I obeyed the Father . . ."

"You rule the universe."

"Yes."

I was grateful to leave the scene and return to the street. Not the Strip, but someplace close.

"And that fifth step," I repeated, "the last one. Is it really necessary?"

"A close friend once called it, the 'Dark Night of the Soul.'"

"But why?"

"It's in darkness that your greatest character will be formed. It's in the darkness of the womb where life blossoms. It's the seed buried in hopeless darkness that sprouts life."

"Hopeless darkness?"

"My greatest champions grow in the darkest places."

I stared hard at the sidewalk. He knew my question and answered before I had the courage to ask.

"Nothing you do will make me love you more, Will. And nothing you refuse will make me love you less."

I felt my eyes beginning to burn. "But," I swallowed. "My love for you, it's so, so intense, so . . ." I choked and tried again. "You said it yourself; you said our hearts are becoming one."

"I know," he gently whispered. Then, even more softly, repeated, "I know."

I closed my eyes, searching for some other way. Any way. But I trusted him. No matter how ugly, no matter how impossible the situation, he was always faithful. Everywhere I looked I saw his love. In my greatest confusion, my worst mistakes, my outright rebellion. There he was with his love. How could I do anything but trust him and return it?

I took a slow, deep breath. And then another. "So . . ." I finally asked, "what's next? Where are we going now?"

"We're already here."

I looked up and saw I was standing in front of a bus station. "Here? What about my flight home? I won't be going home?"

"Not yet."

"Then where? Where am—" I caught myself and looked over to him. "Let me guess, I'll know when I get there."

He grinned. "See how well you know me?"

I looked back down, shaking my head with a sigh.

"Excuse me," a voice called from behind us. I turned to see a homeless man bundled in a heavy sweatshirt and frayed coat. He set his bulging, plastic bags on the sidewalk, so he could pick up a piece of paper. "You dropped this."

"I don't think so," I said.

"Sure, you did." He reached over and handed it to me.

I read it and scowled. "A bus ticket?"

"Don't look like it's been used."

I read the destination. "Briarwood? Where is Briarwood?"

He chuckled. "Ain't no city, I'll tell you that. Nothin' there—less you count the scorpions and snakes. Better hurry, though." He motioned to a bus. "Looks like they're gettin' ready to leave."

I turned to the idling bus, then to Yeshua. But of course he was gone.

That's when I saw the sunset. It had just dropped behind the mountains and was blazing in radiant shades of gold. Above that was orange, then streaks of pink smearing into lavender. The surrounding clouds were on fire in reds and purples. God on Photoshop.

"Beautiful, ain't it," the man said.

"Yes," I agreed.

"Funny. The sun, it blazes all day long, lightin' up everything. But only when it's gone, when the darkness comes, do we really get to behold its glory."

I nodded. *Glory.* He was right. There was no better word for it. But when I turned back to agree, like Yeshua, he was gone. I heard the bus start forward and turned, "Wait!" I shouted. I began running toward it. "Wait for me!" The bus rolled to a stop and the doors hissed open. I thanked the driver and climbed on board. Then, pausing on the steps, I looked back one final time—to behold the glory . . . and pray.

Soli Deo gloria

Seer
Rendezvous with GOD
Volume Five

DISCUSSION QUESTIONS

CHAPTER ONE

1. In striving to make Jesus Christ accessible as the friend, brother, and co-heir he calls himself, I run the risk of making the relationship between Yeshua and Will too casual. That's why the comment about the Mount of Transfiguration (and its scene earlier in the series). How do you deal with the balance of him being the all-powerful Creator of the Universe and the tender Bridegroom?

2. Are there times you address him differently? When?

3. What are your feelings for the way Will has interpreted seeing the Holy Spirit? If your brain were to interpret his visual form, how would you see him?

CHAPTER TWO

1. Do you have similar issues with praying out loud as Will?

2. How do you overcome them?

CHAPTER FOUR

1. Why wasn't the woman healed?

CHAPTER FIVE

1. What specific ways have you seen people misusing the Sword of the Spirit?

2. Yeshua talks about the first steps in growing into all God dreams we can be. What ways have you encountered the first step—God's call and purpose on your life?

3. What ways have you encountered the second step—discouragement by those closest to you?

CHAPTER SEVEN

1. What specific ways do you worship the Artist by admiring his handiwork?

2. Does worship always make you feel closer to God?

3. What do you do when you don't "feel" like worshipping him?

4. How do you approach the "sacrifice" in this verse:

"Through Jesus, therefore, let us continually offer to God a sacrifice of praise." (Hebrews 13:15)

CHAPTER EIGHT

Lots to unpack in this section . . .

1. How do you determine the difference between your will and God's?

2. Since our bodies are the temple of the Holy Spirit, do you agree with the concept that today our Holy of Holies resides in the deepest recess of our soul and is the best place to commune with him?

3. What is the difference between the above concept and the New Age teaching that we are God?

4. What are your thoughts about man-made humility which steals Christ's glory by insisting we're still lowly worms? Is it true that type of humility puts us on the wrong side of the cross?

CHAPTER TEN

1. Can you think of an example today when Christians have done God's work their way instead of his?

2. And now, closer to home, can you think of a specific instance in your own life where you've done that?

3. Does immediate success or failure indicate God's way versus our way?

CHAPTER ELEVEN

Years ago I was asked to fill in to host Jerry Falwell's TV show. While in makeup I asked the staff about the man (who at the time could be controversial). Any prejudice I had melted away as they told me story after story of a compassion few ever saw. His taking time out of his busy schedule to visit a hurt soccer player from his school was such a story. It's always interesting to see what famous Christians are (or are not) like when no one is watching.

CHAPTER TWELVE

1. Obeying God doesn't always bring immediate positive results. I often think of a scene in the movie *It's a Wonderful Life* where Jimmy Stewart gets punched in the face immediately after praying to God for help.

2. Think of a time obedience brought negative results. Has or will positive results ever come about from it?

CHAPTER FOURTEEN

1. Regarding persons, teachings, or experiences, how do you parse counterfeits from the real?

2. What would be a good example of Jesus's teaching:

   "By their fruit you will recognize them. Do people pick grapes from thornbushes, or figs from thistles?" (Matthew 7:16)

3. I'm also a big fan of not jumping to conclusions too soon and pulling out wheat that my limited judgment thinks are weeds:

> *"The servants asked him, 'Do you want us to go and pull them up?' 'No,' he answered, 'because while you are pulling the weeds, you may uproot the wheat with them. Let both grow together until the harvest. At that time I will tell the harvesters: First collect the weeds and tie them in bundles to be burned; then gather the wheat and bring it into my barn.'"* (Matthew 13:28–30)

CHAPTER FIFTEEN

1. Do you agree that Jesus had to rely on the same power source (the Holy Spirit) we have available to us today?

2. Scripture is full of verses stating it was the power of God who raised Jesus from the dead and not Jesus. Here, in Romans it's even more explicit:

> *"And if the Spirit of him who raised Jesus from the dead is living in you, he who raised Christ from the dead will also give life to your mortal bodies because of his Spirit who lives in you."* (Romans 8:11)

CHAPTER SIXTEEN

Holiness versus grace is a wonderful paradox incorporating the heart and mind of God far greater than I can conceive.

1. Has there been or are there currently times in your life when you use Christ's forgiveness as a doormat to simply wipe off your sins so you can continue sinning?

2. Have there been times when God, in his love, has allowed you to keep sinning?

3. Have there been times, in his love, when he's decided it's best to call you into deeper holiness by disciplining you?

CHAPTER EIGHTEEN

Over and over again Scripture commands us to be holy. We're also encouraged not to judge those who fail but:

> ". . . consider how we may spur one another on toward love and good deeds . . ." (Hebrews 10:24)

That said . . .

1. How do we spur without judging?

2. Is there an instance where you've been too lenient?

3. An instance where you've been too harsh?

4. How do you know when to call someone out (or "up") and when to remain silent?

CHAPTER NINETEEN

The word *hypocrite* means actor.

1. Can the phrase, "Fake it until you make it," apply to Christians who are trying to do right but fail? If so, how? How not?

2. Is there a specific time where you've seen the gospel discredited because of someone's hypocrisy.

3. Have you ever been guilty of hypocrisy? If so, what did you do about it?

CHAPTER TWENTY

Patricia makes an interesting statement that if a candidate says they're Christian they should be voted into office.

1. What's your opinion?

CHAPTER TWENTY-TWO

1. Does our culture put too little emphasis on hell? If so, why or why not?

2. How do we discuss hell without negating Christ's love and mercy?

3. How did Christ do it?

CHAPTER TWENTY-THREE

1. Why do you think Will hears the tourists crying, "Feed me!"?

2. What are they starved for?

CHAPTER TWENTY-FOUR

1. Is Will being too hard on Trevor?

2. How do we know when to speak up and when to be silent?

3. Have you ever been in this position? How did you handle it? Did it work?

CHAPTER TWENTY-FIVE

Writing this section brought me to tears—the idea I could actually help Jesus. We see at least two sections in the Gospels where Jesus is racked with emotion. What I wouldn't give to travel back to that time and comfort him.

1. Does that make Jesus Christ too weak? Why or why not?

2. What sort of things can we do today to ease his sorrow?

CHAPTER TWENTY-SEVEN

1. Like Will, have there been times when your obedience makes absolutely no sense?

2. What were the short-term reactions?

3. What do you suppose will be the long-term and eternal reactions?

CHAPTER TWENTY-EIGHT

1. How would you explain the concept of God's "severe mercy" to others?

2. Have you seen his severe mercy applied in your own life?

3. Have you seen him apply it in other lives?

Sneak Peek from:

WARRIOR

Rendezvous with GOD
Volume Six and Conclusion

CHAPTER TWO

THE DRIVER CAREFULLY worked the bus across the rocky desert floor until we were back on the highway. There was plenty of talk and chatter over what happened, but no one felt comfortable enough to share it with me—chalking it up to coincidence or figuring I was a nutjob—or both. Only the man beside me felt inclined to speak.

"Well. Hey, now. That was somethin', weren't it?"

I nodded and was grateful he pried no further. Even more grateful that within fifteen minutes he was back to snoring.

Another two hours passed before we reached my stop. Well, where my stop should have been.

"This is it?" I asked the driver as I stood at the door staring out at the unlit intersection. "Briarwood?"

"Just up that road, not far. Normally, I'd take you, but I don't want to risk it with the roads washed out and all. Had enough excitement for one night, wouldn't you say?"

If he only knew.

"Really ain't a town, though. Just a couple trailer homes, bar, and a rock shop."

He said nothing more, obviously waiting for me to exit. I took my cue and stepped down onto the cracked asphalt. The doors hissed shut, perhaps a bit too quickly, and the bus pulled away, even quicker. Not that I blamed him. I'd have done the same—if I could.

With no luggage, I patted my pocket for the security of my cell phone and started off. The air was warm, smelling mostly of dirt and sand. It took forever for the sound of the bus to fade. When it did, I noticed the stillness. No hum of distant traffic. No buzz of insects. Not even a breeze. Just . . . silence. So absolute it was unnerving. The only sound was the crunch of gravel and sand under my feet—so loud it made me feel like an intruder.

There were no streetlights. Not even some glow from a distant city on the horizon. But it wasn't needed. With the storm gone, a handful of clouds remained overhead—cotton balls with rims glowing bright from the hidden moon. And beyond them, stars, thousands of them. Those closest to the moon dimmed because of its brightness, but the others blazed with pinpoint sharpness. There was more than silence here. There was stillness. So sublime I half-expected Yeshua to join me. The longer I walked, the more I anticipated it—and the greater my disappointment.

He talked about something called the "Dark Night of the Soul." He said it was the final step in making men and women of faith. A time when the seed of his promises fall to the earth dead and buried. It happened to Abraham when he was about to sacrifice Isaac. Joseph when he was abandoned in prison. Jesus on the cross. And in each and every case it was in direct response to their obedience. Not exactly the rewards program Christians are so quick to advertise. And yet, after all I'd been through, I figured a little special dispensation was in order.

Apparently, it wasn't.

Forty minutes later, I saw a fork in the road.

"Okay," I whispered, "which way, now?"

Knowing his fondness for giving last-minute instructions, I continued to approach. But when I arrived, he still hadn't answered. I slowed to a stop. "A little help here would be appreciated."

There was no response.

"I'm trying to obey here. Just tell me what to do."

Silence.

"Anything? A clue?" I waited. And waited some more. "A sign? Nothing big. I'll take anything."

I got nothing.

"What more do you want? I've done everything you've said. Just show me. Is that too much to ask?"

Apparently, it was.

"Alright. You want me to just stay here, is that it? Just stand in the middle of the road and wait? Okay, fine I'll do it."

And I did. For nearly an hour—until the silent stillness began to taunt me.

"Okay, fine." I turned and arbitrarily started down the road to my right. "If this is wrong, stop me, okay? Do whatever it takes to let me know." I kept walking. "Anything. Just tell me."

But he didn't. Was I being too impulsive? Maybe. In the past he pointed out my binary thinking—demanding an *A* or *B* answer, when in reality it was *oranges*. I slowed then stopped. "I'm just trying to do the right thing. What do you want? Was I supposed to take the other one; is that where you'll show me?" With a heavy sigh and not waiting for an answer (why bother), I traipsed the twenty yards across the sandy ground, and past who knows what was hiding there, to the other road. "Is this it?"

Nothing.

"Show me!"

No clue.

No surprise.

I began walking this other road. Walking and fuming. "Alright, fine! I ask, over and over again, and you say nothing. So I'm choosing this one. And if I'm wrong, if it leads nowhere and I wind up dying out here in the wilderness, you only have yourself to blame. Alright?"

After a few steps I slowed, giving him one last chance. "Nothing? Okay, fine!"

I resumed walking.

CHAPTER THREE

I'M NOT SURE how long I walked. Long enough for my petulance to become obvious to me. And embarrassing. The good news was, over the months my temper tantrums seemed to come less and less frequently. Maybe I was growing up. More likely, I was just getting tired of always having to apologize when God proved himself.

God proving himself? To me? What arrogance. Why he insisted on staying with me was a mystery. And yet, it seems the only times he got angry were when I refused to see myself as he did. "I don't make junk, Will," he said. "I would never die for garbage, so stop it with the false humility."

False humility. When he first said that I thought he meant my humility was fake, that I pretended to be humble when I really wasn't (which was certainly true enough). But that's not what he meant at all. He was saying my humility, itself, was a lie. Despite what was obvious to myself and others, I was *not* a world-class loser. I was created in his image. *Imago Dei* he called it. My falseness was thinking I was some lowly, bottom-feeder—refusing to believe I was a child of God. Even worse were the times I secretly felt Yeshua's dying for me wasn't enough to forgive all my failures. And, if it was, he did so under grudging obligation. Finally, there was this whole business of raising me to be his co-heir—of actually sitting on his throne and ruling with him? The very thought was ultimate pride and presumption. But they're his words, not mine.

Of course, when you get down to it, it really is about him, isn't it? By lifting me up he's the one who gets the glory. Talk about a martial arts move. He takes my every failure, no matter how ugly, and flips it around to *his* glory. What a concept.

What a God.

I'm not sure how long I walked before it was clear I'd headed the wrong direction. I'd easily passed what the bus driver said was "just up the road." Of course, I wasn't thrilled about the idea of backtracking and I let Yeshua know—already forgetting my recent repentance for petulance. (Some habits die hard.) I began turning around when I spotted a dark form hidden amidst the white, moonlit rocks nearly a hundred yards off the road. A building? I turned from the road to investigate.

Having no idea what desert creatures lurked behind the rocks, cacti, and whatever else was out here, I watched my every step. As I approached, a small cabin came into view, one end of the roof sagging. The closer I drew I saw it was a patchwork of brown, weathered planks, old plywood, and rusted sheets of corrugated metal. The door was painted bright red. To its left was an opening for a window with only a hanging fragment of glass. There were no vehicles, car tracks, or footprints.

"Hello?" I shouted and was surprised at the loudness of my own voice. "Hello?" I didn't expect an answer but at the same time I didn't want to startle anyone who might be asleep—particularly if they were a lover of loaded guns. "Is anybody here?"

No answer.

I cautiously approached the door making as much noise as possible. "Anybody home? I'm a little lost out here." To my relief, I noticed half an inch of sand piled against the bottom of the door sill. Still, exercising my world-famous bravery, I continued jabbering while reaching for the door to knock. "Not trying to break in or anything. Just need to—"

I was interrupted by a scream (sadly, my own) as a sudden flurry exploded overhead. I ducked as a giant eagle, or tiny sparrow—the distinction made little difference—flew out from under the eve and into the night. Once the attack was over, I rose, checked my pants for dampness, and knocked.

Still nothing.

"Okay, I'm opening the door now." I reached to the corroded handle, a piece breaking off in my hand, and pushed. It took three more tries before the door gave way and scraped loudly across the dirt floor. The good news was there were no further attacks—though I could have done without all the quiet scamperings across the floor.

I pulled out my cell phone and turned on the light. An Airbnb this was not. In the center of the small room sat an old-fashioned, pot belly stove. To my right was a rusted bedframe complete with a tattered and stained mattress. Stacked against the back wall were a handful of wooden crates on their sides acting as shelves—probably for food and supplies—which the mice or rats or whatevers seemed to have enjoyed—except for the dozen or so canned goods in faded labels.

Only then did I notice the smell of coffee. Freshly brewed. I turned the light to my left. Under the window in the moonlight sat a wooden table and chair. On the table rested a large stack of papers. Tablets. I moved to investigate, taking the four or five steps necessary to cross the room. They were legal pads—brand-new. On top was a box of unopened pencils and a small, hand-held pencil sharpener. And beside it was a mug of coffee, its steam rising and sparkling in the moonlight. I had to smile. It seems even the "Dark Night of the Soul" couldn't prevent his love from reaching out to me.

Behind the stack of tablets was an open Bible. Another thoughtful gesture—though considering the app on my phone, it was a bit old school. I moved my light over to see an underlined verse. It was in Hosea. I leaned in to read it just as my light dimmed then flickered out, the battery dead.

Previous Praise for Bill Myers's Novels

Blood of Heaven

"With the chill of a Robin Cooke techno-thriller and the spiritual depth of a C. S. Lewis allegory, this book is a fast-paced, action-packed thriller." —Angela Hunt, *NY Times* best-selling author

"Enjoyable and provocative. I wish I'd thought of it!" —Frank E. Peretti, *This Present Darkness*

Eli

"The always surprising Myers has written another clever and provocative tale." —Booklist

"With this thrilling and ominous tale, Myers continues to shine brightly in speculative fiction based upon biblical truth. Highly recommended." —*Library Journal*

"Myers weaves a deft, affecting tale." —*Publishers Weekly* The Face of God

"Strong writing, edgy . . . replete with action . . ." —*Publishers Weekly*

Fire of Heaven

"I couldn't put the *Fire of Heaven* down. Bill Myers's writing is crisp, fast-paced, provocative . . . A very compelling story." —Francine Rivers, *NY Times* best-selling author

Soul Tracker

"*Soul Tracker* provides a treat for previous fans of the author but also a fitting introduction to those unfamiliar with his work. I'd recommend the book to anyone, initiated or not. But be careful to check your expectations at the door . . . it's not what you think it is." —Brian Reaves, *Fuse* magazine

"Thought provoking and touching, this imaginative tale blends elements of science fiction with Christian theology." —*Library Journal*

"Myers strikes deep into the heart of eternal truth with this imaginative first book of the Soul Tracker series. Readers will be eager for more." —*Romantic Times* magazine

Angel of Wrath

"Bill Myers is a genius." —Lee Stanley, producer, Gridiron Gang

Saving Alpha

"When one of the most creative minds I know gets the best idea he's ever had and turns it into a novel, it's fasten-your-seat-belt time. This one will be talked about for a long time." —Jerry B. Jenkins, author of *Left Behind*

"An original masterpiece." —Dr. Kevin Leman, best-selling author

"If you enjoy white-knuckle, page-turning suspense, with a brilliant blend of cutting-edge apologetics, Saving Alpha will grab you for a long, long time." —Beverly Lewis, *NY Times* best-selling author

"I've never seen a more powerful and timely illustration of the incarnation. Bill Myers has a way of making the gospel accessible and relevant to readers of all ages. I highly recommend this book." —Terri Blackstock, *NY Times* best-selling author

"A brilliant novel that feeds the mind and heart, Saving Alpha belongs at the top of your reading list." —Angela Hunt, *NY Times* best-selling author

"Saving Alpha is a rare combination that is both entertaining and spiritually provocative. It has a message of deep spiritual significance that is highly relevant for these times." —Paul Cedar, Chairman, Mission America Coalition

"Once again Myers takes us into imaginative and intriguing depths, making us feel, think and ponder all at the same time. Relevant and entertaining. Saving Alpha is not to be missed." —James Scott Bell, best-selling author

The Voice

"A crisp, express-train read featuring 3D characters, cinematic settings and action, and, as usual, a premise I wish I'd thought of. Succeeds splendidly! Two thumbs up!" —Frank E. Peretti, *This Present Darkness*

"Nonstop action and a brilliantly crafted young heroine will keep readers engaged as this adventure spins to its thought-provoking conclusion. This book explores the intriguing concept of God's power as not only the creator of the universe, but as its very essence." —Kris Wilson, *CBA* magazine

"It's a real 'what if ?' book with plenty of thrills . . . that will definitely create questions all the way to its thought-provoking finale. The success of Myers's stories is a sweet combination of a believable storyline, intense action, and brilliantly crafted, yet flawed characters." —Dale Lewis, TitleTrakk.com

The Seeing

"Compels the reader to burn through the pages. Cliff-hangers abound, and the stakes are raised higher and higher as the story progresses—intense, action-shocking twists!" —Title Trakk.com

When the Last Leaf Falls

"A wonderful novella . . . Any parent will warm to the humorous reminiscences and the loving exasperation of this father for his strong-willed daughter . . . Compelling characters and fresh, vibrant anecdotes of one family's faith journey." —*Publishers Weekly*

Rendezvous with God

"Gritty. Unflinching. In your face. Emotionally wrenching. *Rendezvous with God* is Bill Myers at the top of his imaginative game. A rip-roaring read you can neither tear yourself away from, nor dare experience without thinking." —Jerry Jenkins, *New York Times*-bestselling novelist and author of the Left Behind series

"A teacher and a storyteller, Bill Myers welcomes, disarms, then edifies in this tight and seamless weave of story and truth. It's innovative, 'outside the box,' but that's why it works so well, bringing the reader profound and practical wisdom, the heart of Jesus, in modern, Everyman terms— and always with the quick-draw Myers wit. Jesus talked to me through this book. I was blessed, and from some of my inner shadows, set free. Follow along. Let it minister." —Frank Peretti, *New York Times*-bestselling author of *This Present Darkness*, *The Visitation*, and *Illusion*

"If you have ever wished for a personal encounter with Jesus Christ, *Rendezvous with God* may be the next best thing. Bringing Jesus into contemporary times, Bill Myers shows us what Jesus came to do, and why He had to do it. This little book packs a powerful punch." —Angela Hunt, *New York Times*-bestselling author of *The Jerusalem Road* series

Insight
9781956454420 – $18
eBook 9781956454437 – $12.99

BILL MYERS

a novel

Insight
Rendezvous with God Volume Four

Commune
9781956454246 – $17
eBook 9781956454253 – $9.99

BILL MYERS

a novel

Commune

Rendezvous with God Volume Three

Temptation
9781956454024 – $16
eBook 9781956454031 – $9.99

BILL MYERS

a novel

Temptation

Rendezvous with God Volume Two

Rendezvous with God
9781735428581 – $16
eBook 9781735428598 – $.99

BILL MYERS

Rendezvous with GOD

a novel